HALFBACK TOUGH

Joe tossed the ball to the referee and began jogging toward the bench. At the ten-yard line, the team crowded around him. Joe was grinning when he escaped the crowd and trotted to the bench. Earl Steel squeezed Joe's arm and said, "Nice play."

Then Joe heard the call—"Hey, Joe baby!"—and there was no mistaking the voice. And there was no mistaking the Joe who was the object of the call. The voice, high pitched and laughing, was Marty's.

Joe turned from the field toward the sound of the voice. There seemed nothing else to do.

"This book is both an exciting sports story and a study of a troubled youth making a critical life choice."
—*Horn Book*

HALFBACK
TOUGH

HALFBACK
TOUGH

THOMAS J. DYGARD

PUFFIN BOOKS

PUFFIN BOOKS
Published by the Penguin Group
Viking Penguin, a division of Penguin Books USA Inc.,
40 West 23rd Street, New York, New York 10010, U.S.A.
Penguin Books Ltd, 27 Wrights Lane, London W8 5TZ, England
Penguin Books Australia Ltd, Ringwood, Victoria, Australia
Penguin Books Canada Ltd, 2801 John Street, Markham, Ontario, Canada L3R 1B4
Penguin Books (N.Z.) Ltd, 182–190 Wairau Road, Auckland 10, New Zealand

Penguin Books Ltd, Registered Offices: Harmondsworth, Middlesex, England

First published in the United States of America by William Morrow and Company, Inc., 1986
Published by arrangement with William Morrow and Company, Inc.
Published in Puffins Books 1989
1 3 5 7 9 10 8 6 4 2
Copyright © Thomas J. Dygard, 1986
All rights reserved

LIBRARY OF CONGRESS CATALOGING-IN-PUBLICATION DATA
Dygard, Thomas J.   Halfback tough / Thomas J. Dygard.   p.   cm.
Summary: New at Graham High, Joe joins the football team and
begins to change his tough guy outlook as he becomes absorbed by the
game and gains self-esteem and new friends.
ISBN 0-14-034113-7
[1. Football—Fiction.   2. Conduct of life—Fiction.   3. High
schools—Fiction.   4. Schools—Fiction.]   I. Title.
PZ7.D9893Ha1   1989   [Fic]—dc20   89-33678

Printed in the United States of America
by Arcata Graphics, Kingsport, Tennessee
Set in Times Roman

HALFBACK
TOUGH

CHAPTER 1

This was the third day of practice and Joe Atkins still could not believe he had actually done it— signed up for football. But here he was, under the searing August sun, wearing pads and a uniform, dripping perspiration, groaning his way through calisthenics with forty strangers on the practice field at Graham High. In front of him the assistant coach, a young fellow named Steve Howard, was barking, "Hup! hup! hup!" With each "Hup!" Joe, his legs spread apart, either bent and touched a toe or straightened back up. The heat was terrible, and the pads were scraping his shoulders.

If only the old gang back at Worthington High could see him now—tough guy Joe Atkins, of all people, sweating through calisthenics with the kind of dudes who played on the football team, the goody-

goody boys who got all the cheers and always walked around like somebody special.

Marty would have laughed at the sight—Marty laughed at everything. He even laughed the day that Mr. Burrows, the principal of Worthington High, caught them taking a nip from a vodka bottle at Joe's locker. Mr. Burrows bounced them out of school for a week for that one. Marty laughed about it. He'd be laughing at Joe right now, stooping and stretching his right hand over to his left toe, the perspiration dripping off his forehead.

Richard would not be laughing. He would be frowning. Richard usually frowned more than he laughed. He was pretty much the leader of the crowd Joe ran with at Worthington High. Richard always seemed angry about something. He would be angry now, seeing Joe in the second row, third from the end, bending and rising at the command of the coach. Joe could hear Richard's words, "Sold out, eh? Gonna try to be one of the snoots, eh? Well, you'll find out." And Richard would not be smiling as he spoke the words. He would be frowning.

But Marty and Richard were not here in Graham. They were back in Worthington, a hundred and fifty-five miles to the west, where Joe Atkins had lived until his father's company promoted him to manager of the Graham office. Joe and his parents had made the move a month ago. Was it only a month? It seemed like years. Joe, knowing no one in Graham, had dragged through the long days alone. He watched television and went to movies. He cut the grass when his father told him to. He washed the car when his father told him to. And he did it all with an empty feeling. He missed the comradeship of Richard and Marty and the other guys in Worthington. He missed it most of all the one time he had called Richard on the telephone. "What are you guys doing?" Joe asked. "Nothing," Richard said, which of course meant they were doing everything they always did—cruising in Richard's car, hanging around Sandy's Drive-In, going out to the beach at Lake Moseley—and along the way kicking up a little trouble.

After that telephone conversation, Joe had asked his parents if he could return to Worthington for his senior year of high school. He was sure he could live with Richard—Richard's parents never bothered to say no to anything. But Joe's parents said no. And they suggested that he not call Richard again. They never liked Richard anyway.

In the afternoons Joe would sometimes walk over to Graham High and sit in the bleachers next to the tennis courts, watching the players. He sat alone. Nobody spoke to him, and he spoke to nobody.

Except, that is, the day he lit a cigarette. Quick as a flash, a boy was in front of him. The boy had a dark tan, which seemed all the darker against the white tennis shirt and shorts he was wearing. His short blond hair looked even lighter above the deeply tanned face.

"No smoking on the school grounds," the boy announced.

Joe glared at him. Who did this dude think he was, the chief of police? Besides, what was wrong with having a smoke? All of Joe's friends back at Worthington lit up cigarettes all the time. There was even an area designated for smoking outside, next to the main school building. Very few of the teachers, and none of the students, ever said a word about smoking—unless it was a joint. And Joe hadn't lit up a joint while sitting in bleachers watching the tennis players. So what was with this dude?

The boy stood in front of Joe, looking him in the eye, neither moving nor speaking.

Joe returned the gaze for a long moment. He considered telling him to go jump in a lake. But instead, with slow and deliberate movements, he took a drag on the cigarette and exhaled a cloud of smoke in the direction of the boy. Then, as if the boy didn't exist, he looked down and dropped the cigarette on the bleacher seat next to his foot and ground it out. He stood up and, looking past the boy instead of at him, turned and left.

Richard would have been proud. Marty would have applauded. But Joe, as he went down the bleacher seats and then across the sidewalk into the street, felt none of the satisfaction that had always come with putting down a goody-goody. For the first time in his new home, Joe had identified himself as a tough guy.

But it hadn't felt good. To his surprise he found himself wondering if perhaps the goody-goody had not come out the winner, and he himself the loser. He frowned as he walked home.

For a couple of afternoons after that Joe skipped the tennis courts at Graham High. He had to cut the grass one of those afternoons, anyway. The other afternoon, the Cubs were playing the Expos on television, and he wanted to watch.

The next time Joe went to the tennis courts to while away an afternoon, the patch of grass between the courts and the school building had been buzzing with activity. Wide double doors in a wall of the building were standing open, and groups of boys were milling around just inside of them. Other boys were still arriving—on foot, on mopeds, on bicycles, and one bunch in a car.

"What's going on over there?" Joe had asked a tennis player sitting in the bleachers a couple of rows below him.

"Football sign-up," the other boy answered, hardly giving Joe a glance.

"Football," Joe said, speaking more to himself than to the tennis player.

"Yeah, football," the boy replied. This time he did not even turn his head in Joe's direction. He was watching the action on the court.

Joe turned his attention back to the players on the court, too, and for a moment he sat with only his head

5

moving—first left, then right, following the ball as the players volleyed. Then he glanced back to his left, beyond the court, toward the boys around the open doors of the field house.

He stood up. "I think I'll go have a look," he said, speaking to no one in particular.

The tennis player below him did not answer or even look around. His head was moving from left to right to left, following the ball.

Joe skipped down the bleacher seats and walked across the grass toward the open doors. As he approached he could see what was happening inside. A long table had been set up just off the end of the basketball court. A skinny boy in a T-shirt and shorts, wearing glasses, was behind it. The T-shirt was emblazoned "Wildcats" in orange across the chest. He was holding a clipboard and passing out little cards to the boys who signed the paper on the clipboard.

Joe stopped at the edge of the open doors and watched. There was a lot of chatter and some laughter. Everyone seemed to know everyone else, and they all seemed friendly with each other. Several boys who walked past Joe glanced at him with curiosity. Joe glared back at them. Nobody spoke.

As Joe watched the scene, for some reason his thoughts went back to the words his father had spoken on their first evening in their new home. "You're in a new town, and it's a chance for a new start," his father had said. "You made enough trouble for yourself back in Worthington to last a lifetime. This move to Graham is a chance for you to leave all of that behind you and start over—a clean slate. Pick the right people for your friends this time, and you'll be better off—and happier. It's up to you."

That was a month ago. Joe had gritted his teeth and sat stone-faced through his father's advice. He had to listen. He had no choice. But what did his father know? Joe had liked his friends in Worthington. He had had fun with them. He had not wanted to leave them behind.

But now the replay of his father's words brought to mind the picture of Joe blowing cigarette smoke into the face of the boy at the tennis courts—and the strange feelings he'd had while walking home afterward.

Joe started to leave, to go back to the bleachers and watch the tennis players some more. But he did not turn and walk away. He stayed rooted to the spot, watching the boys mill around the sign-up table, calling out greetings to each other, laughing and talking.

Joe had considered going out for football at Worthington High last year. But only briefly. Richard scoffed at the idea. "Do you really want to be one of that bunch of snoots?" he had sneered. Marty laughed at the idea and said, "It's more fun getting drunk under the bleachers than getting your head busted out on the field." Joe dropped the idea.

At the time, though, he had weighed his chances of

making the team; and now those questions popped back into his mind.

Was he fast enough? Sure. He had run on the track team in the ninth grade, and had won most of his races. And the night the cops surprised the gang while they were spray-painting the wall of Mr. Bennett's hardware store, who was the only one fast enough to get away? Joe Atkins, that's who.

Was he strong enough to play football? Well, he was stronger than Richard and Marty and any of the others, and they all admitted it. Marty even hung the nickname "Muscles" on him for a while.

Was he tough enough? *Tough*? Tough was Joe Atkins's middle name. Richard and Marty were probably still talking about the fight after that basketball game with Morton Tech. Joe mopped up the place with the wise guy from the other school until the cop working the game got there and broke it up.

Joe had shrugged his shoulders slightly as he completed the mental appraisal of his ability to play football. He did not consciously decide to walk across the floor to the sign-up table. He did not ask himself if he wanted to sign up for football. He simply found himself at the sign-up table, suddenly looking down into the face of the skinny boy with glasses.

"Yeah?" the boy had asked.

"I want to sign up."

"You're new."

"Yeah, just moved to Graham this summer." Joe

frowned at the skinny boy as he spoke. "What is this," he thought, "a federal case? Why all the questions? Is it a crime to be new in town?" He started to turn and walk away.

Then the skinny boy grinned at him. "Didn't think I had seen you around," he said. "Here, sign up—name, height, weight, position, all of the stuff—and I've got a card for your locker assignment and equipment."

Joe did not return the boy's smile. He nodded curtly, as if accepting an apology. He took the clipboard from the boy and picked up a yellow pencil with a long string attaching it to the clipboard. He printed carefully on the next vacant line: Joe Atkins, six feet tall, one hundred and seventy-five pounds, and—

Position? Joe frowned again. What position did he play? He did not know. But he hesitated only a second, aware that the boy was watching him. He wrote: halfback.

"Okay," the boy said. He looked down at the sheet on the clipboard and then added, "Joe." He handed Joe a card. "You're number forty-two. You'll find your locker and get your gear"—he pointed across the basketball court—"through that door over there."

Joe nodded, turned, and started walking in the direction the skinny boy had pointed. He felt funny, almost light-headed. He did not want to admit it, but he was excited. This was going to be good. His father, for sure, would be pleased, and Joe guessed that was okay. Richard would scoff and Marty would laugh, but they weren't here.

Through the door, Joe found himself in the locker room—rows and rows of lockers, with benches in front of them—and off to the left, the entry to a shower room. To his right, a young man stood alongside a table laden with gear—shirts, pants, shoes, socks, pads. He was wearing a T-shirt labeled "Coach" and a whistle dangled on a cord around his neck.

"Here," the man had called to Joe. "Over here with your card."

Joe walked over and handed the man the card.

"You're new."

"Yes," Joe said. This time he did not take offense.

"I'm Steve Howard, assistant coach," the man said.

"Joe Atkins." Then he added, "From Worthington."

"I see. Okay, give me your sizes . . ."

Joe tried to remember everything—waist, shoe size, all of it—and each time he made a guess Steve Howard loaded him down with something else.

When he had finished, Steve Howard said, "Number forty-two is over that way."

"Uh-huh," Joe said, glancing in the direction of the coach's nod. Then, peering over the top of his arm-load, he headed for his locker.

Suddenly, a player, already dressed in his practice

uniform, came around the end of a row of lockers. Joe was looking at the stenciled numbers on the lockers and did not see him. They collided.

"Sorry," the player had said, reaching out to help Joe keep from dropping his armful of gear.

Joe recovered his balance without dropping anything and looked at him.

It was the dude—deep tan, blond hair—who had told him he could not smoke a cigarette on the school grounds.

Steve Howard blew his whistle, a shrill shriek that seemed to cut through the hot afternoon air like a knife. "All right! All right!" he shouted, his face thrust forward toward the rows of players. "Enough loosening up. Now let's get to work."

Joe, on his back, pulled himself into a sitting position, grateful that the leg lifts were at an end. He held the sitting position, sneaking in a moment of rest.

"C'mon, Atkins! On your feet!"

Joe glanced at Steve Howard as he scrambled to his feet. It was not a friendly glance. His legs ached as he forced his body up, and his shoulders ached when he moved them. Joe wiped his forehead with the sleeve of his sweatshirt and looked down at it. The sleeve was wet. He looked up at the blazing sun.

"I must be crazy," he told himself.

CHAPTER 2

"All right! All right!" Steve Howard was barking again. "Backs and ends at this end of the field and linemen at that end. Get a move on. Let's go. We're going to find out what you can do."

The young assistant coach had seemed nice when he was handing out equipment on sign-up day. But from the first moment he and the players met on the practice field, all pleasantries vanished. He did not look at the players; he scowled at them. He did not speak to the players; he snapped at them. The easy smile was gone, replaced by an ever-present frown. Directing the calisthenics that opened each day's practice session, he reminded Joe of the Marine Corps drill instructor he had seen in a movie back in Worthington early in the summer. He was mean. That was the only word for him.

The Graham Wildcats' head coach, Earl Steel, remained a puzzle to Joe. He was an older man but the name Steel fit perfectly. He was thin, almost bony, and shorter than Joe, but he looked hard as steel. His blue eyes were cold, hard, and unblinking. Even his hair, cut short, was the color of steel—a frosty gray. He neither smiled nor frowned. He seemed, rather, always to be calculating something. He never shouted at anyone. In fact, he never said much at all. But he popped up everywhere on the practice field—under the goalposts when Joe was finishing wind sprints, next to him during the calisthenics, in the middle of the backfield when he and the other players were walking through plays.

Joe had spoken with Earl Steel only once, on the field during the first day of practice.

"You're Atkins," the coach said. "From Worthington."

"Yes."

There was a pause. Joe figured the coach was waiting for him to add, "Sir." Joe didn't.

Steel looked him over for a second. "Did you play football at Worthington?"

"No," Joe said. "Well, some sandlot, you know. Not varsity."

Steel nodded. "Worthington is in our conference, you know. We'll be playing them. You'll get to play against some old friends."

Joe did not count a single football player at Worthington as a friend. But he said, "I guess so."

Steel studied Joe for another moment and then walked away.

Joe almost grinned at the coach's back. "Now what was that all about?" he asked himself.

In the opening days of practice Joe began learning the names of the other players. The dude—deep tan, blond hair—was Paul King, the quarterback. Paul obviously remembered Joe with the cigarette and, as Joe had intended at the time, he did not like what he remembered. Paul said nothing to Joe, but—well, that was just it: he said nothing to Joe. "Okay by me," Joe told himself. "Let the snoot have it his own way." But Joe figured Paul had told all his friends. A lot of the players—Chuck Slater, Dave Horton, Jason McNeal, and some others—were treating Joe with indifference or suspicion. They hung around in groups, usually around Paul King, making inside jokes among themselves and giving out with buddy-buddy talk. Joe didn't mind. He was pretty good at ignoring people himself.

A couple of the players went out of their way to be friendly to him. Andy Walker, the fullback, a short block of granite with a baby face and a mop of black curly hair, grinned a lot and shouted encouragement at Joe. Cramer Springer, a tackle, walked over and introduced himself to Joe on the first day of practice. "Welcome to Graham," he said, sounding like he meant it. Joe could not help liking the grinning face of

Andy Walker, and he appreciated Cramer Springer's words of welcome and firm handshake.

The player Joe watched the most—and the one who watched him the most—was Jason McNeal. Joe and Jason both were listed as halfbacks on the typewritten roster posted on the bulletin board in the corridor outside the locker room. A lot of other players were listed as halfbacks, too, but Joe learned quickly that Jason McNeal was the one he had to beat out for a place in the starting lineup.

"Ol' Jason is worried about you," Andy had said to Joe with a grin in the locker room after the first day of practice.

"Jason who?"

"Jason McNeal. He was second-string flanker last year behind Spike Traynor. Spike graduated. Jason figured he was a cinch to win the job this year. But now there's a new name on the list—you—and he's not so sure."

"Which one is Jason McNeal?"

Andy was still grinning. "The one who's watching you."

Joe followed Andy's gaze to a boy with reddish hair who was staring at him. Joe returned a cold-eyed grin—the same kind of grin he'd given the wise guy from Morton Tech just before the fight. Joe always fought to win, and now he was out to win the starting flanker position. And he figured that Jason McNeal knew it.

* * *

If Joe kept telling himself that he was crazy to kill himself in the hot August sun—and for what?—there was one person who thought it was great: his father. In fact, his father used exactly that word.

Joe and his parents were at the dinner table the evening of sign-up day when Joe made the announcement. "I'm going out for football," he had said without preamble. "I signed up today."

There was a moment of silence. Then his father said, "That's great. Absolutely great. It's a good way to meet people."

Joe gave his father a quick glance. He knew what he had meant. Football was a good way to meet the "right" people, not those like Richard and Marty, with their cigarettes, vodka, and trouble.

"Yeah," Joe said, "I'm sure to meet my teammates, that's for sure."

"Get the lead out!" Steve Howard shouted from the end of the field. "Let's go! Let's *go!*"

Joe, walking toward the end of the field, sighed and broke into a trot. Steve Howard never let up. Not for a second. Joe jogged silently alongside Paul King toward the group of players gathering around the assistant coach.

Howard glowered at the team members surrounding him. "Well," he said finally, the sarcasm fairly dripping, "so you're the ones who say you are the backs and ends—the skill positions." He dragged out the word—"skil-l-l." He must have liked the way it sounded because he said it again. "The skil-l-l positions."

Some of the players glanced around at each other uneasily. Standing next to Joe, Paul King stared at Steve Howard without moving, giving it the old Jack Armstrong, all-American boy, jut-jaw treatment. Joe could have laughed.

"We've been playing around so far," Howard continued. "A little bit of exercise. A little bit of running. A little bit of walking through plays." He paused, looking at the players around him. "But now we're going to get down to work. We're going to find out who wants to play. And we're going to see if you've got all the skill-l-l that you think you've got."

Joe wondered how he ever could have thought that Steve Howard was nice.

"Gimme a center," Howard bellowed, and a muscular boy—Joe knew his name: Charlie Janis—peeled away from a group of linemen lunging at each other and ran across the field.

The drill was simple. The center bent over the ball. The quarterbacks—Paul King and a couple of other boys—stood behind him. The backs and ends divided themselves into two groups, then queued up, one line to the left of the center and one to the right. The quarterbacks took turns reaching under the center, taking the snap, backpedaling and passing—first to a receiver coming across from the left, then to one cutting across from the right.

It was a quick-moving drill. Somebody always was throwing, somebody was always running. A ball was in the air, going somewhere, almost all the time. But for Joe and the others standing in line, more time was spent waiting their turn than running out for a pass. And as he idled in the line, Joe watched the quarterbacks.

He had to admit that Paul King looked good. He took the snap and backpedaled from the center like a dancer. He cocked his arm and passed in one smooth movement—a quick release of the ball. His passes zinged to the mark like they were on a clothesline. No loft, no wobble, and right on target every time. The other two quarterbacks were nowhere near the class of Paul King.

Some of the receivers looked better than Joe had expected. A lanky end named Matthew Jefferies loped out for a pass with a deceptive appearance of laziness. He seemed hardly to be moving, much less exerting himself. But all of a sudden there he was—far out there—reaching up to bring in the ball. Joe was impressed. He was impressed, too, by Jason McNeal's performance. The first time out, Paul King sent a whistling bullet pass at Jason that seemed sure to knock him over. But Jason reached out and took in the pass without breaking stride. Joe's right eyebrow went up a notch.

Joe's turn came. He had not drawn Paul King. He

did not know the name of the quarterback crouching behind Charlie Janis and barking the signals—"Hup ... hup ... hup."

Joe took off on the third "hup," the snap signal. He ran about five yards straight ahead. Then he angled to his left, over center, going deeper all the time. He looked back and saw the ball coming—high, a wobbler, off its mark, too far out in front of him. He shifted into high gear. The ball was coming down. At the last moment he lunged and got the fingers of his right hand on the ball. He batted the ball gently up to keep it in the air somehow until he got himself under it. The ball floated upward. Joe felt himself starting to tumble in the headlong rush. Then he regained his balance. The ball was coming back down. Joe got both hands on the ball. He pulled it in.

As he turned to throw the ball back to the student manager who was collecting them for the center, somebody in one of the lines cut loose with a shrieking whistle. Somebody else applauded. It was Andy Walker.

Joe felt like grinning back at Andy. The catch had felt good. He knew, too, that most receivers would never have gotten a hand on the ball, much less have pulled it in. But when Joe Atkins turned on the afterburners, he was fast. And his hands had not let him down. He had shown them—Paul King, Steve Howard, all of them. And what did you think of that, Jason McNeal? But Joe did not grin.

Jogging and then slowing to a walk, he took his

place at the rear of the line on the opposite side to await his next turn. He felt Steve Howard's eyes on him, but he stared straight ahead—into the steel-blue eyes of Earl Steel, watching from his position next to the lunging linemen at midfield. He had seen the catch.

"Great catch," Andy Walker called out, leaning out from his position a couple of spots ahead in the line.

"Thanks."

Next time up, Joe drew Paul King.

Joe sprung off the line at the sound of the third "hup." He dashed five yards straight downfield, then veered to his right, angling over center.

As Joe made his cut, he looked around. The ball was right there—too early. His mind flashed a question—on purpose? But no, the ball was not exactly there, it was a shade behind him. Off-target—on purpose? Joe reached up and behind him, just above the shoulder, just off his ear. The bullet pass thunked into his hands and he grabbed hard. He was sure for a second that the ball was going to zip through his hands. But he held on.

"How's that, smart guy?" he said to himself as he brought the ball in and tucked it away. "Right on target with ol' buddy Jason, weren't you? But a little early and a little off target with Joe Atkins's pass."

He sent a shovel pass to the student manager and trotted to the end of the line.

The quarterback who had sent Joe a wobbly pass

on his first outing already was taking the snap for the next throw. Somebody was racing out, watching, arms extended.

Paul King was standing back, awaiting his turn to throw. He turned and walked across to Joe at the end of the line. "Bad pass, sorry," he said. "Good catch. You saved it."

Joe looked at Paul, and his mind flashed the question again—on purpose? Joe didn't know. He nodded an acknowledgment to Paul.

CHAPTER 3

By Saturday, the day of the first full-speed contact scrimmage, Joe figured he was on his way to locking up the starting flanker position.

Beginning with the passing drill on Wednesday, he had outshone Jason McNeal at every turn. He was sure of it. He had displayed good speed, more than Jason McNeal. He had made the tough catches, more of them than Jason McNeal. Now in the scrimmage he was going to prove that he ran against tacklers—real tacklers, not stand-up defenders in a dummy scrimmage—with more toughness, more strength, and more determination than Jason McNeal.

Then when the Fullerton Eagles came to Graham next Friday night for the season opener, the starting flanker for the Wildcats was sure to be Joe Atkins. Jason McNeal, Paul King, and all of those snoots may not like it. Tough luck. They were going to know Joe Atkins's name, even if they never used it. They were going to have to admit that he existed, even if they did keep looking at him like he was a creature from Mars or something.

In truth, Paul King had been nice, polite, proper, almost friendly the last couple of days. Joe was willing to admit it. Paul always said, "Nice catch," or "Good play," when Joe pulled one off. But Joe figured Paul King was always nice, polite, proper, almost friendly. Joe knew the type. Teachers loved them and parents pointed to them as examples. But while Paul King was saying what he was supposed to say and acting like he was supposed to act, he always seemed to be looking down his nose at Joe, about to leap forward to tell him, "No smoking allowed on the school grounds." The remembrance showed on Paul's face every time he turned to Joe and said, "Nice play." Joe could see it written there.

What cracked Joe up was the way the others, even Jason, chimed in, "Nice play," after Paul King said it. Nobody ever spoke up until Paul King said it first. Then they knew it was okay. Joe could have run on his hands and caught the ball with his feet, and nobody would say a word until Paul spoke. Joe almost laughed at the sheep following Paul King's lead.

Only Andy, and sometimes Cramer, spoke up on their own without waiting for Paul to show the way. Andy, always smiling, didn't seem to care what Paul or anyone else thought. And Cramer, for all his ferocity in the blocking drills, seemed earnestly intent on being everyone's friend.

But none of that mattered. The big things were his running, his receiving, and—today—his performance in the first full-speed contact scrimmage.

Joe crossed the street and broke into a jog when the school came into view. He could hardly wait. He wanted to get going—into his uniform, onto the field, catching passes, running with the ball. He trotted up to the door and went inside. Across the basketball court he saw Andy Walker's back, topped by the thick mass of curly black hair. Andy disappeared into the corridor leading to the locker room. Joe walked around the edge of the basketball court and turned into the corridor.

Down the corridor, Andy and some of the other players were staring at a piece of paper thumbtacked to the bulletin board. Joe walked over and squinted at the notice from the back of the crowd. It was the division of the squad—the lineups—for the scrimmage: two offense units and two defense units that would take turns playing against each other.

Joe scanned the lists and found his name.

Then he blinked and looked again. He could not believe his eyes. He was listed with the second-team backfield. On another list were the names Paul King at quarterback, Andy Walker at fullback, Chuck Slater at running back, and, unbelievably, Jason

McNeal at flanker. Joe was listed at flanker with the quarterback who threw wobbly, off-target passes, a fullback who couldn't block a butterfly, and a running back with the speed of a crippled turtle.

Joe felt his face flush red. He took a step backward. He was sure everyone was looking at him, watching for his reaction, enjoying his shock. Somewhere in the back of his mind he heard Richard's voice. "See," he was saying, "the snoots will get you every time, if you let 'em. You've got to figure out who your friends are." In Richard's book, even Earl Steel and Steve Howard, who drew up the assignments, qualified as snoots. They were teachers, weren't they? And didn't the teachers always take care of the snooty students? So Earl Steel and Steve Howard had taken care of Jason McNeal and had made Paul King happy. Tough luck, Joe Atkins.

Joe looked around. Nobody was paying any attention to his reaction. They were too busy searching out their own names and those of their friends. Joe thought about turning and leaving, just walking out, never to return. Who needed these guys?

Then Andy's baby face, with that unruly mess of black curly hair and the wide smile, loomed in front of him. "Don't think a thing about it," he said.

Joe glared at the grinning face. "What?" he asked.

"I said, don't think a thing about it," Andy repeated. He was still smiling.

"A thing about *what?*" Joe asked. His words came

out in a snarl and his lips were curled slightly in an ugly expression he had not worn since leaving Worthington. "What do you think you are, anyway—a mind reader or something? What makes you think that I'm thinking anything about anything?"

Andy, by moving to his right, turned Joe away from the others in front of the bulletin board. The players were beginning to watch and listen.

"C'mon," Andy said softly, his smile gone. He turned and walked several steps down the corridor. Joe followed him.

"I can tell you what they're doing—if you'll listen," Andy said.

"What do you mean?"

"They're putting Jason—"

Joe, thrusting his face close to Andy's, cut him off. "What makes you think I care where they put Jason?"

Andy looked at him without speaking. For a moment Joe was sure that Andy was going to walk around him and head for the locker room, leaving him alone in the corridor.

Speaking softly and looking at the floor instead of into Andy's face, Joe said, "Yeah, I care."

"Cool off," Andy said. "It may all be for the best."

Joe looked at Andy and waited.

"Look at it this way," Andy said. "Jason played second string last season behind Spike Traynor, who graduated. Jason's earned a shot at the flanker job. He earned it last season. It's his job—until somebody beats him out of it. The coaches are giving him every chance to hang onto the job. He's entitled to the chance. He's earned it." Andy paused. "Look, everyone knows you've got him whipped by a country mile. So what's it going to hurt giving him this chance?"

Joe watched Andy, then looked away. He had to admit that his words made sense. But Joe was having trouble swallowing them. The fact remained that the snoots had squeezed him out. So what were Andy's words worth? He was probably one of them, anyway.

Joe looked back at Andy, half expecting to see a sneer of satisfaction on his face—"the salute of the snoots," as Richard called it. But Andy was not sneering. He was watching Joe intently, a slight frown replacing his usual grin.

"It's only a scrimmage," Andy said. "And our first scrimmage, at that. It's not like a regular season game or something."

Joe nodded. "Yeah," he said.

"Besides, like I said, it may all turn out to be for the best."

"I don't see—"

"If you go out there and tear 'em up, playing with that bunch in your backfield—and your line isn't so hot either, in case you didn't notice—you're going to come off looking twice as good."

"Uh-huh. I guess so." Then Joe managed a smile. "Sure," he said.

"Good, then let's go. Okay?"

Andy started around Joe, heading for the door to the locker room.

"Wait a minute," Joe said.

Andy stopped. "Yeah, what?"

Joe looked at Andy in silence for a moment. He was not sure the word would come out. But he got it out. "Thanks," he said.

Andy shrugged and grinned and walked on toward the door with Joe following him.

The scrimmage was nearing the end of its first fifteen-minute period. The Paul King offense was on the field, nearing the finish of its first stint.

Earl Steel was on the field in the midst of the players. He was acting out the roles of referee, coach, critic, and—sometimes, but only rarely—cheerleader. On every play, he had his head stuck in one huddle or the other, listening to the signals in the offense huddle or eavesdropping on the play-calling in the defensive huddle. He was at the point of the ball at the end of every play, lecturing, dissecting, praising, criticizing.

A smattering of fans—parents, friends, idle onlookers—stood scattered along the edge of the field, their hands shielding their eyes from the blazing sunshine. Joe, standing at the bench, spotted his father across the field, then turned his attention back to the action.

Steve Howard's shrill whistle stopped the movement on the field. The first fifteen-minute period was at an end and the first-team offense left the field. The defense stayed on to play a second period. Joe and his teammates jogged onto the field.

Earl Steel picked up the ball and marched to the forty-yard line, plunked it on the ground, and nodded toward the second offense unit.

The players gathered in the huddle. The quarterback, Fred Robertson, knelt on one knee and leaned into the huddle. Joe remembered Fred's wobbly and off-target passes.

Fred called a running play, sending the fullback over tackle. Then he sent the fullback over guard. Then he sent the running back around right end.

On each of the running plays, Joe's mission as flanker was to move out in a buttonhook pattern, posing as a receiver, and maybe draw some of the defense away from the runner. Being a decoy was boring work. Joe wanted to carry the ball.

At the end of the series of plays, Earl Steel marched the ball back to the forty-yard line.

In the huddle again, Fred was about to open his mouth when the coach suddenly appeared. Steel barked one play, then another, and withdrew from the huddle without waiting for acknowledgment. This time out the plays would all be passes, with Joe the primary receiver. Fred nodded unconsciously and repeated the first play, and they broke the huddle.

Lining up, Joe stared at the defenders facing him—the Wildcats' first-team defense unit—and tried to appear casual, ready for nothing more than the decoy's role again.

With the snap, Joe loped straight ahead for eight paces, then swung his shoulders to the right, trying to lure the cornerback into committing himself. The cornerback was a real eyeball watcher, though, and paid no attention to Joe's shoulders. The fake did not work. But then Joe looked to the right, and the cornerback took the bait. Joe pivoted and headed left. He was free and angling deeper downfield.

He counted the steps after the cut ... three, four, five ... and looked back over his shoulder.

The ball was in the air. It was wobbling—Fred's trademark—but it was coming. Joe slowed his pace a bit. The ball was falling short. He cut back slightly to meet it.

Joe grabbed the ball with both hands. He heard the dreaded hoofbeats of a tackler bearing down on him. Tucking the ball away and cutting sharply, he reversed his field. He saw the blur of a tackler flash by out of the corner of his eye. Then he shifted into high gear and did not stop until he crossed the goal line.

Turning in the end zone, now with the ball on his hip, he looked back up the field and saw Earl Steel. Steel had his hands on his hips, and his face was thrust forward, staring at Joe.

Some of the players at the bench and a few of the onlookers stretched out along the other sideline sent up a cheer. Joe grinned as he jogged upfield and returned the ball to Earl Steel with a shovel pass.

Back in the huddle, Fred said only, "You've got the play," and repeated the signal Earl Steel had directed.

Joe lined up and stared into the eyes of the defensive back. He did not know the boy's name, but he knew one thing about him for sure: he had a little less faith in eyeball-watching than before. He had taken Joe's fake.

Fred took the ball from the center and moved to his right, faking a handoff into the middle of the line. The linemen, and even one of the linebackers, were charging.

Joe moved out—one step, two, three—and pivoted in front of the cornerback. The cornerback, cautious now, was left behind when Joe turned to his left, toward the center of the field, and raced parallel to the line of scrimmage five yards deep. Joe was alone.

Fred stopped, straightened up, looked, cocked his arm, and threw the ball.

Joe, bent low and running at full speed, turned and looked. The ball was coming. Probably Fred had put everything he had on the pass. But it wasn't much. The ball was coming at Joe with something less than zip. It was floating. But it was on target. Joe reached for it. So did a linebacker, coming across. The linebacker's hand nicked the ball and it bounced up. It seemed to hang in front of Joe, and he lunged forward. The ball was dropping. Joe bent lower as he ran, reaching out for it. He caught the ball at knee height. He kept lunging forward. Head down, he bumped into somebody. Joe spun away from the tackler, and was free. He could feel it. But only for a second. Then something like a two-ton truck smashed into him from behind and drove him to the ground.

When the two-ton truck had removed itself, Joe leaped to his feet and looked at the sideline marker. He had gained ten yards on a deflected pass that most receivers never would have touched.

Then he saw Earl Steel standing in front of him. His heart sank. He knew what was coming. He had lowered his head and blindly run into someone. All week the coaches had been exhorting ball carriers to keep their heads up and their eyes open. Ten yards or not, he was going to catch the wrath of Earl Steel.

"Young man," Steel said.

"Yes," Joe said.

"When Paul King's team returns, stay on the field at flanker for a little while, will you?"

Joe blinked at the coach in surprise. "Yeah, sure," he said finally.

"I want to see if you're for real," Earl Steel said. Then he turned and walked away, beginning his march back to the forty-yard line with the ball.

CHAPTER 4

When Steve Howard's whistle sounded the end of action for the second-string offense, Joe trooped halfway off the field with the players. Then he stopped and waited to join the first-team unit coming on. For a second or two he was left standing alone on the field, his helmet dangling in his right hand. He felt foolish. He was sure everyone was looking at him and saying he was showing off, standing there alone.

And he felt a bit nervous, too, as he awaited the arrival of the first-team offense. He had been playing with the second team and had outclassed them all. The great catches were all his. After the first two, he had caught two more, one of them for another touchdown. The touchdown was a fluke. The long pass, sailing high—a floater—had interception written all over it. But the defensive back got his feet tangled and fell down. Joe, like a baseball outfielder, just stood there and waited for the ball, caught it, and ran across the goal. A fluke, sure, but still a touchdown. The one great run of the period was his, too—a twenty-seven-yard gain on a double reverse. He simply out-ran everyone until a cornerback came across and shoved him out of bounds. For sure, he had been a star among the second-stringers. But now came the first team. They were better. So he—Joe—should be better. The thought was a little scary.

Paul King led the first team back onto the field. Joe watched them coming, and found himself searching the faces for Jason McNeal. Maybe Joe had misunderstood Earl Steel. Maybe Jason was supposed to be taking the field and Joe was to go to the sideline. Then he really would look the fool. But he did not find Jason's face in the crowd of players approaching him. He spotted Jason on the sideline. He looked gloomy. Somebody was talking to him, and he was nodding his head.

"Ready, Joe?" Paul King asked, and then ran on past him without waiting for an answer.

Joe turned and followed Paul and the others to the huddle. He could not remember Paul ever calling him by name before.

At the forty-yard line, Earl Steel was standing over the ball, impassively watching the players draw themselves into a circle.

Paul stood in the huddle, hands on knees, and

looked around at the circle of faces. Joe watched him and then, feeling a pair of eyes on him, glanced at Andy. Andy grinned at him and winked. Joe looked back at Paul.

"Let's give them a shocker," Paul said. He called for a long pass. Joe, racing down the sideline, was the primary receiver. If Joe were covered, the pass would go across the field to Chuck Slater moving out of the backfield.

They broke the huddle and Joe, lining up at the flanker position, eyed the new defensive back facing him. Joe knew the face from practice, but not the name. The defensive back danced nervously from one foot to the other. His case of nerves was understandable. He had spent the previous fifteen-minute period on the sideline watching Joe Atkins leave all defenders in his wake. Joe took a deep breath and remembered Earl Steel's words: "I want to see if you're for real."

Paul took the snap and rolled out to his right. A strong runner, Paul always offered the threat of a quarterback keeper play. Andy, circling out ahead of Paul, presented the threat of a pitchout. The defensive linemen reacted with caution. So did the linebackers.

Joe took off at full speed without the bother of a fake and ran past the defensive back. The defensive back spun and raced in pursuit.

At the twenty-yard line, Joe looked over his shoulder and saw the ball coming. He sensed rather than saw or heard the defensive back chasing after him. The pass, a perfect spiral, was going over Joe's head and he pushed with all he had. The ball was coming down. He stretched forward and reached out. He thought he was going to catch the ball. But it skittered off his fingertips and fell to the ground. Joe, lunging forward at the final instant, lost his balance and tumbled to the ground.

"My fault," Paul said in the huddle. "Bad pass. I led you too much."

Joe, puffing, nodded. He meant the nod as only an acknowledgment of Paul's statement. Then he thought the nod might be interpreted the wrong way, as agreement that Paul had thrown a bad pass, that the failure was all Paul's fault. True, the pass was a few inches off the mark. But Joe did not want to give the impression that he felt that any incompletion had to be the passer's fault. He said, "I'll take one more step next time."

"Can you do it again? A rerun right now would catch them off balance. Can you?"

"Uh-huh," Joe puffed. He wasn't sure. But he had to try.

"Sure?"

"Sure."

Paul nodded. "Same play," he said to the players around him, and they broke the huddle and fanned out into their positions.

Joe lined up, breathing heavily—even more heavily than he had to. The act might convince the defensive back that he was in no shape for another sprint down the sideline. The heavy breathing might leave the other player believing that any movement out of Joe was nothing more than a distraction. If it worked, Joe was going to gain a couple of steps on him. And he needed those couple of steps. He was not going to have the same spring in his legs this time.

Paul rolled to his right again with the ball in his hand. Andy was running ahead of him, looking back, appearing ready to take a pitchout. Chuck sprinted toward the left sideline. Joe took off down the right sideline.

Joe raced past the startled defensive back, crossed the twenty-yard line, and looked back over his shoulder. The ball was coming. It was right on target. Joe put up his hands. The ball settled in. Joe tucked it away and ran across the goal.

From there, four running plays into the line left Joe more an observer than a participant. He ran patterns designed to slow down the charge of the linebackers or to stall the defensive backs. Andy, strong as a bull, slammed into the middle of the line twice, dragging tacklers with him for gains of seven and nine yards. Chuck Slater, a tricky runner and stronger than he looked, skipped around end for a nine-yard gain. Paul kept the ball on a rollout and cut back over tackle, gaining five yards behind a strong block by Cramer Springer.

Joe was impressed. He had watched from the side-line during the first fifteen-minute period on the field, and had admired the work of the first-team offensive unit. But now, being in the middle of the action on the field, was different. He saw the tiny—but critical—things they did to gain one more yard, two more, or freedom to the goal. Chuck Slater was a master of the change of pace. Paul's fakes were brilliant. Once, he almost turned a linebacker completely around with a shoulder fake. Andy's stiff-arm work with his left arm got him almost as much yardage as his powerful legs. Cramer Springer and the other linemen mauled the defense time after time. Joe had speed. He had good hands. But he knew he did not have the highly polished basic skills of the others.

In the huddle, Paul called the short pass over center—Joe, going three steps ahead, was to cut sharply to his left and run parallel to the line of scrimmage, five or six yards deep. It was the same play that Joe had run with Fred at quarterback, catching a deflected floater.

"It'll come in low," Paul told him, and then added with a grin, "but not as low as last time."

"Uh-huh. Okay."

At the snap, Joe ran straight ahead ... one step, two, three ... keeping his eyes on the defensive back fading in front of him.

He tried a fake to the right, fooling no one, then pivoted and raced to his left, five yards behind the line of scrimmage. He looked back. Paul was up high. He might have been off the ground, leaping. He released the ball high. Joe saw it coming, a whistler, zinging down in front of him. He extended his hands waist high and felt the ball smack into them. He grabbed hard. For a moment he was sure the hard-thrown spiral was going to tear its way through his grip. He remembered the velocity of the first Paul King pass he had caught three days ago. He grabbed harder and held on.

Somebody bumped him hard on the hip. He felt a hand slide down his leg as his forward lunge carried him away from the tackler. He had the ball. He tucked it away.

Joe cut sharply to his right, upfield, where the yards were to be gained. Something hit him on the hip. He felt arms locking around him. He spun furiously. The arms fell away. He ran again. Somebody hit him high, on the shoulders. He ducked and got away. He was still running. Then, one, two—low and high—a pair of tacklers had him. He strained to fall forward, trying to carry the tacklers with him. It might mean another yard, maybe two. He fell.

When the tacklers got off him, Joe sprang to his feet. In front of him he saw Andy getting up from a block. His teammate was grinning at him. "Pretty tough running," Andy said. Joe, winded and hurting in the hip where he had been belted twice, said, "Yeah, tough." Then he added, "Thanks." Paul appeared out of nowhere and began clapping Joe on the back and shouting, "Nice running." Joe nodded. "Thanks."

Earl Steel, picking up the ball to return it to the forty-yard line for the next play, turned to Joe. "Take a rest," he said, gesturing toward the bench. And then, hardly loud enough to be heard, speaking as if it were almost an afterthought, he added, "Nice work." Without waiting for an acknowledgment from Joe, he turned to the sideline and shouted, "McNeal!"

Joe turned and began walking toward the sideline, removing his helmet as he went.

The applause started somewhere off to Joe's left, among the onlookers strung out from the end of the bench to the goal line. Joe paid no attention at first. But then the applause spread along the sideline, growing in volume. Joe noticed it now. He looked up. Everyone along the sideline was looking at him and clapping their hands—onlookers and players alike—as he walked off the field alone, his helmet held in his right hand. Joe stared at the scene. Then he looked at the ground and broke into a jog toward the sideline and a seat on the bench.

Joe Atkins, tough guy, did not know what else to do.

"See, what did I tell you?" Andy Walker asked, coming out of the showers with a towel looped around his waist. He was giving Joe a baby-faced grin out from under a soaking-wet mop of black hair. "Didn't I tell you?"

Joe was heading into the showers. He had been delayed in a happy way. Players who never had spoken to him had been coming up to offer their congratulations. Players who did not know him were introducing themselves. Players who had been only faces with no names were shaking Joe's hand. Joe said, "Thanks . . . thanks," more times than he could count.

He grinned back at Andy. It was hard not to grin at Andy. Besides, right now Joe felt like grinning at the whole world. "Yeah," he said. "Yeah, you were right."

Then Joe stepped into the showers. He was alone. Everyone else was in the locker room, toweling off and dressing. He stood, turning slowly, enjoying the needles of hot water pounding on his body. He thought back over all those nameless faces that had been smiling at him and calling him by name and telling him what a great job he had done. These guys didn't seem so bad, not bad at all. He remembered the times that Richard and Marty—and, yes, Joe Atkins, too—had scoffed at the football players at Worthington High. They were "jocks," "head-knockers," "heroes." Pronounced just the right way, the words dripped with sarcasm. Richard was particularly good at pronouncing the words just the right way. But these guys, these football players, seemed okay.

Jason was not among those congratulating Joe. But

no big deal. That was to be expected. Joe Atkins was going to send Jason back where he had spent last year, sitting on the bench. Paul King had not come around for a handshake in the dressing room, either. Oh, sure, he had clapped Joe on the back in the excitement of the moment after Joe's tough running. And he had said, "Nice job," when he jogged past Joe on the way to the dressing room at the end of the scrimmage. But that was all. Maybe he thought he ought to hang back with his buddy Jason. More likely, he just thought he was too special to say anything more.

Joe stepped out of the shower, grabbed a towel off the table, and began drying himself as he walked to his locker. A dozen players were left scattered around the locker room, putting the finishing touches on dressing.

Earl Steel intercepted him. "You okay?" the coach asked.

"Sure." Joe was surprised by the question.

"You took some real licks out there."

"I'm okay."

Steel looked at Joe for a moment without speaking. Then he said, "Okay," and turned away. As he did, he added, "Nice work out there today."

Joe said, "Thanks," but he was speaking to the coach's departing back.

CHAPTER 5

The week leading up to the season opener against the Fullerton High Eagles got under way with a startling surprise that set Joe Atkins off on a new and strange path.

The sports section of Sunday's Graham *Journal,* presented to Joe by his father at the breakfast table, blared the headline:

Flying Newcomer Sparkles
In Graham Scrimmage

The first paragraph of the story beneath the headline read: "A bolt of lightning named Joe Atkins stole the show in the Graham Wildcats' first full-speed contact scrimmage yesterday. A transfer student from Worthington High, Atkins combined flying feet, sure hands, and tough running to ..."

Joe blinked as he read the words. In his mind, he saw again the icy gaze of Earl Steel watching him, only barely revealing approval, and heard again the coach's softly spoken words of praise. He heard again the applause of the onlookers and the players as he walked off the field. He felt again the handshakes and the backslaps in the locker room.

A photograph, two columns wide and about six inches deep, pictured Joe—arms outstretched, head turned to look back at the ball. The caption read: "Flying Joe Atkins pulls in a Paul King pass for a touchdown."

This was not the first time Joe had seen his name in the newspaper. Last spring the Worthington *Gazette* identified him as the other occupant of the car when Richard was arrested for drunken driving. They both had been pouring down vodka and Richard, kidding around, was intentionally weaving his car from side to side on a darkened road. Suddenly a car with a flashing red light on top appeared. Richard was eighteen years old, and the public notice of arrest was proper. But Joe was only seventeen, a minor, and the editor of the newspaper called on the telephone and apologized for the error in naming him. Joe had barely been able to hold back the chuckles when first his father and then he accepted the editor's apologies. Later, he and Richard both doubled over with laughter when he told his friend about the call.

This was different—and felt better.

He thought of Richard and Marty and the old days back at Worthington—so very different from this moment—and wished he didn't have to play against his old school. Oh, sure, it would be fun to smack the snoots who never had given him a second glance. This time the jocks at Worthington wouldn't be able to avoid Joe Atkins. But Richard and Marty and some of the others were sure to be there, and for sure they'd be heckling their old friend, for all to see.

Joe laid down the paper and looked at his father, beaming at him across the breakfast table.

"You're famous," his father said with a chuckle.

Joe couldn't help wondering if his father, too, had remembered the last time Joe Atkins's name was in a newspaper. That time, instead of standing along the sideline watching his son play football, he had had to get out of bed and come to the jail to sign him out. His father had said nothing that night, but his silence was worse than a scolding lecture.

"Huh, yeah, famous," Joe grunted. He knew better than to let his guard down. He had learned that lesson a long time ago. One newspaper clipping back at Worthington hadn't ruined his life. And one clipping in Graham wasn't going to fix him for life, either.

But when Joe and his parents attended the late services at Saint Matthew's Episcopal Church, several of the churchgoers pointed him out. When he sat in the bleachers and watched the tennis players that afternoon, people stared at him and some of them nodded to him when their eyes met. And when he stepped up to the ticket booth at the Graham Theater in the evening, the boy inside asked him, "Are you Joe Atkins?"

Joe was surprised at every turn—when people looked at him, pointed him out, nodded to him, or spoke to him, just like he was somebody important.

That night in his room, before turning out his light and going to bed, he glanced again at the newspaper, now laid out on his chest of drawers. The headline and the photograph leapt out at him. He had a funny feeling—funny, yes, but good.

At school registration on the Tuesday following Labor Day weekend, everyone at Graham High— students and teachers alike—seemed to know the newcomer named Joe Atkins. Total strangers called out, "Hi, Joe," in the corridors. The teachers smiled at him and said, "Good morning, Joe."

Being known was not a new experience. The students and teachers at Worthington High, and the people around town, too, knew Joe Atkins. He could see the recognition in their faces when he walked by. But not many of them spoke to him. "Snoots," Richard always said. "Let 'em go. Who needs 'em?" The teachers had kept a watchful eye out when Joe and his friends were around. They always seemed to become more alert, and to frown a lot. Joe and Richard used to laugh about it.

But this was different. The teachers at Graham High were not frowning at Joe, they were smiling.

They did not go on the alert. They seemed relaxed and pleased at having seen him. And instead of glancing at him and then looking away, the students grinned and called him by name. Different, really different.

Joe began smiling back at everyone. He had not done much smiling at Worthington High. He and the others in his crowd laughed a lot, usually at the things nobody else found funny. But they seldom smiled. What was there to smile about? School was a drag, the teachers were boring or downright mean, and the students were snoots or dumbbells. But now Joe was smiling back at people. He couldn't help it. And the smiles felt good.

At practice, in the classroom and corridors, around the house in the evening, the world began to seem like a happy place.

On the practice field, the sessions went well. The buddy-buddy backslapping mood of the locker room, so prevalent after the Saturday scrimmage, had cooled down. But Joe wasn't surprised. He figured it was bound to taper off. He couldn't expect everyone to burst into applause and try to shake his hand every time he caught a pass. But he always was working with the first-string backfield—Paul and Andy and Chuck—and that was the important thing. Paul still pranced around like he thought he was something special. He seemed hardly to speak to Joe, except in the line of duty. Maybe he resented him for knocking

Jason out of the starting lineup. But Joe shrugged off Paul's snooty attitude and paid no attention when his teammate walked past him without speaking. He had seen snoots before.

Earl Steel added to Joe's string of pleasant surprises when he picked him out of the line early in the passing drill on Wednesday and took him aside. "I want to see you field a few kicks," he said.

For twenty minutes Joe stood alone along the sideline and fielded kicks—first the towering spiral punts and then the tumbling place kicks. He caught them all without a bobble. Each time, he moved under the ball, brought it in, tucked it away, jogged a few steps, and turned to see Earl Steel staring at him without changing expression.

Finally, Steel said, "Okay. That's enough." He walked up to Joe. "You're going to be it Friday night."

"It?"

"Punt returner and kickoff returner."

Joe just nodded. But he felt his heartbeat quicken.

As the week wore on toward the Friday night game, Joe found other surprises.

He was surprised by the new way he approached his classroom work. Joe sat straight in his seat. He did not think about it; he just did it. Back at Worthington High, he and Richard and Marty had always slouched, legs stretched out into the aisle. The posture never failed to spark a reaction—first, there was a sharp order from the teacher to pull those feet back under the desk; second, everyone in the classroom turned to stare; third was a slow movement to comply; fourth came laughter from a couple of the students in the class.

He watched his new teachers with a serious face, and he listened to what they said. He did not decide to watch and listen; he just did it. Back at his old school, he had ignored the teachers except when they forced him to pay attention. He read magazines until they were taken away from him. He wrote notes and passed them to Richard and Marty until the teachers wised up and separated them. He spent a lot of time gazing out the window. Once, he dozed off in class. It got a real laugh from everyone except the scowling teacher.

Now Joe completed his homework assignments each day, either in study hall or at home after the long afternoon of practice. He did not decide to study, he just did it. Back at Worthington High, Joe had dawdled his way through the study hall periods and never—never—taken a book home for work at night. Once, when Joe and Richard made a wager on which of them could make the lowest grade on a test, Richard turned in a blank sheet of paper with his name at the top, smirking in the certainty he had won the bet. But Joe, with a blank sheet of paper, misspelled his own name. Richard admitted that Joe won the bet.

In the course of the week Joe even began to take on

a different appearance. He did not decide to change; he just did it. He combed his hair, cleaned his fingernails, and washed his hands. His clothing took on a tidiness that would have astounded the old bunch back at Worthington High.

If his parents noticed the changes in Joe, they said nothing.

The players might have noticed Joe's transformation. He had been unkempt, scowling, and surly on sign-up day, and remained little better during the week leading up to the first full-speed scrimmage. Now he was neatly groomed and smiling. But none of the players said anything.

And neither did Joe.

By Friday afternoon, free of practice because of the night game coming up in four hours, Joe was whistling softly when he walked out the front door of Graham High and headed home.

He could hardly wait for the game.

CHAPTER 6

Joe stood on the sideline watching the Wildcats' captains, Paul King and Cramer Springer, march to the center of the field for the referee's toss of a coin. He shifted his weight nervously from one foot to the other. Unconsciously, he jiggled the helmet held in his right hand. He wished the game would get under way. Then maybe the nervousness would go away.

Under the glare of the arc lights, the field was a bright green carpet of manicured grass with white grids marking the yardage lines. Players on both sides of the field stood at the sidelines watching their captains—the Wildcats in orange uniforms with black trim, the Fullerton High Eagles in white with crimson trim. The bleachers behind Joe and across the field in front of him were packed with shirtsleeved fans wait-

51

ing in the warm September evening for their teams to open the season.

The Fullerton High Eagles looked big enough and numerous enough to Joe, and not at all like the small school with the undermanned team that Earl Steel seemed so fearful his Wildcats would consider them to be.

All week long, Coach Steel had issued warnings about overconfidence. Sure, he conceded, Fullerton High was a smaller school than Graham High. But watch out, he cautioned. Sure, Fullerton High lacked bench strength—and lacked skill, too, at some positions—but watch out. Sure, Graham High had trampled the Eagles 42–0 in the opener last season. But that was last season. This was a new season, so watch out.

Joe figured that maybe the coach had good reason to fear overconfidence. The Wildcats, traditionally opening their season against the Eagles before heading into their conference schedule, had not lost to Fullerton High in more than ten years. Usually, the score was a whopper. And on Thursday, Cramer Springer had jokingly asked the coach, "If we get ahead by forty points, can I run a few plays from fullback?" Earl Steel glowered at his standout tackle. When Andy kept referring to the game as a warmup for the conference season, Steel glowered at him, too.

But Joe, standing at the sideline and wearing a game uniform for the first time in his life, was finding it difficult to muster up a feeling of confidence, much less overconfidence. His heart was pounding. His hands were sweaty. The roar of the crowd from both sides of the field just made things worse. All those people were watching. The cheers sounded somehow different from the ones he had heard when he and his old friends were under the bleachers having a smoke and a swallow of vodka before a game.

At the center of the field the referee flipped the coin into the air. Somebody called the toss—heads or tails—and everyone watched the coin fall to the ground. The four players and the referee bent over to look at it.

The referee straightened up and gestured. The Graham High Wildcats had won the toss. They would receive the opening kickoff.

Joe's heart beat even faster, even harder. The first-ever play of Joe's first-ever game was going to find him standing alone, awaiting a kickoff, with all eyes on him. He had not dared allow himself to hope the Wildcats would lose the toss of the coin. That would amount almost to treason. But he had been unable to keep out of his mind the thought that it might be nice—really more comfortable—to begin the game as one of eleven players jogging out to huddle up. He glanced down the field, where he would be standing to receive the opening kickoff. He clenched his left fist into a tight ball, then opened the hand and wiped the sweaty palm on his jersey.

Paul and Cramer were jogging back to the bench, heading for Earl Steel. The other players were gathering around the coach. Joe moved over to join them.

His teammates were jumping around slapping each other on the shoulder pads and shouting. The eruption of noise from the mob of players was deafening. Earl Steel's mouth was working but Joe could not hear the words. The roar from the bleachers, where all the people were on their feet, rolled in on top of the Wildcats' shouts. Then, suddenly, the group of players broke up. Eleven of them trotted onto the field and the others spread out along the sideline in front of the bench.

Joe jogged onto the field with the other starters, then peeled away from the group and veered to his left. He jogged all the way back to the fifteen-yard line and stood there alone. Joe never had felt so alone in all his life. All eyes were on him. He was sure of it. He took a deep breath. Mrs. Allison, the speech teacher back at Worthington High, always said a deep breath helped cure nervousness. But it didn't help much. Joe wiped his sweaty hands on his thighs and waited, staring straight ahead.

The Fullerton High kicker moved forward toward the ball. Flanking him on both sides, and a couple of yards behind him, his teammates moved forward. The kicker planted his left foot and swung his right one. The ball went high. Then, tumbling end over end, it began coming down. Joe, his head back, watching the flickering image in the arc lights, took a step to his right, then a step forward.

All the coaches' words during the last few days raced through Joe's mind. Earl Steel had said, "The first thing you've got to do is catch the ball. If you don't catch it, nothing else matters." Steve Howard had said, "Don't start running until you've caught the ball. The worst mistake is trying to take off too early." And: "A fumbled kickoff is the most disastrous play in football."

Joe wanted to wipe his sweaty palms again. But there was no time. The ball was coming down.

"Run straight up the middle," the coaches had told him. "Run into the crowd. Your blockers will try to get you through to the other side of the crowd, into daylight."

Daylight? But this was nighttime. The totally irrelevant thought danced through Joe's brain. He almost smiled at the little joke. But there was no time. The ball was here.

"Catch the ball," he told himself. "First thing, catch the ball."

Joe gathered in the tumbling ball. It was no different than all the kickoffs he had received in practice. There was no difference at all.

He tucked the ball away, then raised his eyes and looked upfield. A white uniform was coming at him from over to the left, ten yards away. Ahead, the orange uniforms of his teammates were clustering in the center.

The Fullerton High tackler was moving in on him

and Joe took off, straight ahead. The tackler flashed past him. He had overshot Joe. With one tackler behind him, Joe headed for the crowd at the center of the field.

The swirling mass of players looked impenetrable. But then something opened—a tiny sliver of a gap—between a pair of orange jerseys. Joe ran for the opening. He bumped his way through, legs pumping hard.

"Head up—keep your head up," one of the coaches had said. "Watch where you're going."

Joe wriggled out from between the backs of his two teammates, looking for another opening. There seemed to be bodies everywhere, most of them wearing orange jerseys. But some of them wore white. There was no opening. If only he had time to find one, or to wait for one. But there was no time. If only everyone would quit moving around. But they did not quit moving around.

Then, to his right, he saw it—nothing, absolutely nothing, but open space. He veered toward the right.

A hand clawed at his shoulder. He jerked free. Another grabbed at his thigh. He pulled away.

A white uniform suddenly filled the open space that Joe wanted. But it was too late to change his route. He took a tighter hold on the ball and, knees pumping high, ran straight for the white uniform.

"Fake with your shoulders," Earl Steel and Steve Howard always kept telling him. "Dip your left shoulder a little, and then run to your right."

Joe saw the Fullerton High player waiting for him—a player now, not just a white uniform. The player, feet spread apart, was dancing a little jig, ready to move left or right to grab Joe, or to take him on head-on. He held his arms spread wide. He was staring into Joe's eyes.

Joe looked to his left. He ducked his left shoulder—only slightly, but maybe enough. Then he cut to his right.

The Fullerton High player was not fooled by the fake and moved with Joe, crouching a bit and waiting for the impact of the tackle.

Then from Joe's left, a blur of orange jersey flashed into view. The Fullerton High player took his eyes off Joe. He turned and raised his hands in defense. But it was too late. He vanished under the crushing block of somebody in an orange jersey.

Joe cut back to the left, behind the blocker knocking the tackler off his feet, and he saw the field empty before him.

He raced to the goal, forty yards away, and circled in the end zone.

Looking up, he saw the wildly waving fans on their feet in the bleachers behind the Graham High bench. He heard the cheers of the crowd—surely the loudest roar he ever had heard.

Suddenly he was surrounded by a mob of players wearing orange jerseys. The whole world was orange. Hands slapped at his helmet, his shoulder pads, his back. He saw some faces—Andy's, Cramer's—but mostly he just saw orange. Somebody jumped on his shoulders in a giant hug, and for a moment he thought he was going to fall.

Then the crowd of players melted away and he jogged toward the bench.

Earl Steel stepped forward. He seemed about to smile. Joe never had seen the coach smile. The coach didn't—but he came close. "Nice bit of running," he said to Joe and turned away, watching Ron Sterling kick the extra point.

From then to the halftime the Wildcats trampled the Eagles mercilessly. The Graham High defense never let the other team cross the fifty-yard line. And the offense, with Andy and Chuck hammering at the line and Paul firing short passes to Joe, rolled down the field with ease. At halftime the score was 35–0.

In the dressing room Joe sat puffing on a bench, winded and leg weary. The defense's outstanding play, always stopping the Fullerton High Eagles cold, had left the Wildcats' offense on the field almost the entire first half. For Joe, being on the field meant running. He had caught four passes. Three of them were short bullets that left him alone with the ball and unprotected, the target of all eleven tacklers on the field for Fullerton High, and he had taken a hammering on each of them. The fourth catch, a twelve-yarder, was in the corner of the end zone for a touchdown.

But even when Joe was not the target of a pass, he ran his patterns, trying to draw the defense away from the ball carrier. He ran as hard when the play sent Andy slogging into the line as he ran when Paul King fired a pass at him.

Beyond that, he was the receiver of each of the Fullerton High punts. He caught them all without a fumble and, as always, ran hard. He gained six, nine, eleven, and twenty yards on the punt returns—not bad, but it was tough work.

Now, slumped forward on the bench in the locker room, his breath coming in gasps, he felt like he had run ten miles.

Earl Steel was standing near the door, saying something. Joe looked up and gazed at the coach.

"Laugh while you can," Steel snapped. He was looking at Andy. The icy glare wiped the smile off Andy's face. Everyone had been laughing and joking. Winning big was a lot of fun and the Wildcats were enjoying themselves. But the coach's words turned the faces serious all around the room. "You're a lucky bunch," Steel said. "You're making mistakes out there—serious mistakes—that another team, a better team, would pick up and jam back down your throats."

Joe sighed. Didn't that man ever let up?

Speaking in a flat monotone, Steel proceeded to recite a litany of errors—missed blocks, an offside penalty that called back an eight-yard run and cost the

Wildcats five yards in penalty, a bobbled handoff, a dropped pass, sloppy tackling.

As he listened, Joe idly turned his head and his eyes fell on Paul King. The quarterback, frowning, was nodding in agreement with every indictment handed down by the coach. He looked as though he thought that none of the criticism applied to him, that he was above it, merely acknowledging the correctness of the coach's assessments of everyone else's shortcomings. Joe recognized Paul's expression—it was the same one he had worn when he popped up and said, "No smoking on the school grounds." Joe snorted to himself.

At the finish, Steel said, "Nobody's got a lock on a first-string assignment on this team. We'll see what the second-string team can do in the second half."

Paul nodded his approval.

"What a snoot," Joe said to himself as he trooped out of the dressing room to spend the second half standing at the sideline, his helmet in his hand, watching the Wildcats wrap up a 49–7 triumph.

CHAPTER 7

For Joe Atkins, the next three weeks flew by.

On the playing field, the Graham High Wildcats rolled over their next three opponents, proving that the flattening of the Fullerton High Eagles had not been a fluke. The Wildcats were a football power-house. With three of their victories coming over Northern Big Seven Conference opponents, they had everyone in Graham—from the corridors at school to the drug stores, barber shops, and cafes in town—talking about winning the championship.

Everyone agreed that the key ingredient of their success was the newcomer named Joe Atkins. He was a reliable target—a receiver with good hands—for Paul King's able passing. And, with the ball in his hands, Joe was a streak of lightning. His speed left most opponents floundering in his wake. When caught, he was hard to bring down. He fought to the last second of every play. He had eight touchdowns to his credit—two on kickoff returns, one on a punt return, and five on passes—and led the team in scoring.

Even without the ball, Joe was a major asset to the attack. His mere presence worked wonders for the Wildcats. Wherever he went on the field, linebackers watched him with care and edged over in his direction. Defensive backs pursued him. The attraction of Joe Atkins opened different routes for the other backs. With the linebacker one step out of position because of Joe, Andy Walker was able to make an extra couple of yards on a plunge through the line. Because a defensive back was keeping one eye on Joe Atkins, Chuck Slater made bigger gains zipping around the ends or knifing off tackles.

For Joe, football was a strange and wonderful—and fun—world that he had never known existed. Somebody was always saying, "Nice catch," or "Good job," and he grinned and nodded at them. He came to enjoy even the grueling practice sessions. The misery in the August sunshine was now only a dim memory. The runs and catches in the games, the roaring cheers of the crowd and the shouted compliments from his teammates—they were thrills. The nicks and bruises were nothing.

Thanks to football, everyone knew Joe off the field—in the classrooms and the corridors of Graham High, and all around town. People honked and waved from passing cars. They came over to say hello when he was having a Coke in Braden's drugstore. A couple of times youngsters asked for his autograph. Joe felt himself blushing as he signed their books, and he hoped no one was watching. However, he had to admit that the sensation of being such a celebrity was pleasing.

Aside from his success on the football field and the local fame that came with it, life for the new Joe Atkins was good. He was actually enjoying his classroom work. He had discovered that paying attention in class and preparing his lessons made life better, not worse. For one thing, he was learning about all kinds of stuff, and some of it was interesting. For another thing, Joe discovered that keeping up with his schoolwork removed the old dread of facing another week, another day, another class with the certain specter of failure looming there in front of him. He learned that success in the classroom was almost—not quite, but almost—as exciting as success on the football field.

In the midst of it all, the old troubles with his father and mother—the hassles and arguments that went on all the time—just seemed to dry up and blow away.

His cautious, tentative friendship with Andy was developing into a strong camaraderie. Ever since Andy cooled him down on the first day of the first full-speed contact scrimmage, Joe had experienced a new and strange feeling about him: trust. Back at Worthington, Joe had considered Richard and Marty and some of the others to be his friends. After all, he hung around with them all the time. But he never entertained the notion of trusting them. It was smarter not to trust anyone. Everyone was out for himself, and the quicker the lesson was learned, the better. But it was different with Andy. When Joe succeeded, Andy cheered. When Joe failed, Andy encouraged him. Andy included Joe in his circle of friends, mainly Matthew Jefferies, the split end with the loping stride. They went places together—the movies, Harry's Hamburger Heaven, everywhere. No cigarettes, no vodka, no trouble, just a lot of fun. Richard and Marty wouldn't believe Andy Walker was for real.

As for Paul King, Joe finally had decided to catch his passes and take his handoffs, and not worry about him. Andy always was telling him, "You just don't understand Paul. He's not so bad." And one day Joe decided to agree with a grin and a shrug and a noncommital "I guess so,"—although he kept the label of snoot attached to Paul King in his mind.

Only one event turned Joe's smiles to a frown. It was on Wednesday during the second week of classes. Joe was at his locker in the second-floor corridor between classes, dropping off a sweater that had become too warm to wear. He glanced at a boy opening the locker next to his. He never had seen the boy before, but he blinked, then gaped. Yes, he *had* seen the boy before. Joe was looking at a mirror image of his former self.

"Hi, Joe," the boy said. The voice carried a slightly mocking tone. The face wore a crooked half-grin that seemed to say, "I know you think you're better than I am because you're big stuff on the football team."

Joe stared without speaking. The mocking tone, the crooked smile, even the uncombed hair and the shirt-tail partly hanging out—it was him, it was Richard, it was Marty, it was all the others in his old bunch back at Worthington High.

Joe wondered if there was a vodka bottle in the locker? A package of cigarettes in the pocket?

His mind flashed back to the corridors of his old school and he saw again his classmates walking past him, giving him a quick glance, then turning away. It all seemed so long ago.

"Hi," he said finally. Then with the eerie feeling that he was looking at himself, he asked, "What's your name?" Joe would not have been surprised to hear the boy reply, "Joe Atkins."

The boy's leer remained in place. "Aw, it doesn't matter," he said, and turned and walked away.

Joe watched the boy's back disappear into the milling throng of students. Then he closed his locker and snapped the combination lock into place. He turned and headed the other way, toward his next class, with an uneasy frown on his face.

* * *

The scoreboard clock was ticking off the final seconds of the game.

Standing at the sideline with the other Graham High players, Joe glanced to his right and saw the numbers in lights on the scoreboard: Graham Wildcats 31, Meadowcliff Ramblers 7. He turned his attention back to the field. Dave Horton, blitzing from his linebacker position, dropped the frustrated Meadowcliff quarterback for a loss.

The Wildcats' fourth straight victory was going into the record books.

The Graham High fans jamming the bleachers on both sides of the field were on their feet cheering when the game ended.

Joe and his teammates turned and jogged to the end of the field, filed through the gate in the chain-link fence, and trotted across the grass to the doors of the school building. As they ran, a multitude of hands reached out and clapped them on the shoulder pads or the helmet. Winning felt good.

For Joe, it had been the fourth standout game. He caught seven passes, one for a touchdown, and scored another touchdown on a punt return. He also logged the game's single longest rushing gain, thirty-one yards, on a double reverse. Yes, winning felt good.

Turning into the locker room, he saw the chalked words on the blackboard—*Worthington Next.* The Wildcats would be traveling by bus the one-hundred and fifty-five miles to Worthington for the game. The words sent a series of images flashing through Joe's mind.

He saw Richard and Marty and the others hanging over the little chain-link fence that separated the playing field and the benches from the bleachers. Joe had been there with them, a little high on vodka, shouting at the players, more than once last year. Were his Graham High teammates going to wonder how those guys shouting at them happened to know Joe so well?

He saw old man McCrory, the biology teacher, who always tried to police the students during the Worthington home games. Joe had heard his squawky voice and seen his forefinger shaking in his face plenty of times. Was old man McCrory going to look at the Graham High Wildcats' lineup and recognize the name of the Atkins boy who had moved away? Or was he going to look out onto the field and see the face he had seen so many times under the bleachers? Was he going to say something to somebody? Old man McCrory just might do it.

He saw the faces of the Worthington players. He hadn't known any of them well, but always recognized them in the corridor. They were the jocks, the heroes. They had paid no attention to Joe, and he paid no attention to them. But some of them were bound to remember him. Were they going to taunt him on the field? "Hey, want a slug of vodka?" Or, "Hey, did you have a cigarette in the huddle?"

Joe saw other faces—an unsmiling Earl Steel, and Paul King wearing an expression that said, "I thought so." He saw Andy, and maybe Matthew, too, saying, "It doesn't matter." But it would matter. And he saw the face of that boy with the locker next to his, whose expression had seemed to say, "Who are you trying to kid? I recognize you. I know your type." And now he would leer and say, "Yeah, I knew all the time about you."

Joe was frowning as he approached his locker and began peeling off his jersey. He did not want to go to Worthington. He did not want to play at Worthington. Why were they in the same conference as Graham? Everything was going great. But now—

Maybe if he caught a cold, or sprained an ankle, Earl Steel would leave him at home. People did catch colds. Players did sprain an ankle in practice. The solution was really quite simple—miss the trip, miss the game, stay at home—and escape all risk.

But no, no, he told himself. Who would catch the passes? Who would return the kicks? Who would run the double reverse? The Wildcats were counting on him. For the first time in Joe Atkins's life, he knew someone was counting on him. Better to have old man McCrory say something, or have one of the players make a crack, or have Richard and Marty show up—better that than running out on the teammates who were counting on him.

"Why are you shaking your head?"

Joe turned and looked into Andy's grinning face. "I, uh, just—"

"We're going to whip your old buddies over at Worthington next week," Andy said. "You're going to like that."

"Yeah, man."

CHAPTER 8

Joe heard Paul call the snap signal—"hup!"—
and he broke from his standing position into a jog for
six steps downfield. Then he curled around and, slowing to a walk, headed back to line up again.

The signal drill, a warm-up exercise in the last minutes before the game, was moving the Graham High
Wildcats down the sideline in the Worthington High
football stadium.

Joe looked around at the familiar scene. Across the
brightly lit field the Worthington High Tigers, in their
royal blue uniforms with gold trim, were moving
down the sideline in their own signal drill. How many
times in past years had he seen players in those uniforms? Behind the Worthington players stood the familiar figure of Coach Gibson McCarthy, trim in the
blue and gold running suit he always wore at the

games. The scoreboard at the end of the field was the same—a clock in the center, "Tigers" in lights on one side and "Opponent" in lights on the other for the posting of scores, all against a background of wavy blue-and-gold tiger stripes. The four-foot chain-link fence, tall enough to keep the crowd back but short enough to spring over if you really wanted to, was still in place around the field. Even the bleachers seemed peculiarly Worthington. How could bleachers differ in appearance? But these seemed different from others, and familiar to Joe. And there in front of them stood old man McCrory. He had his back to the playing field and was staring at someone up in the bleachers. And straight ahead in front of Joe, beyond the goalposts opposite the scoreboard, stood the red brick school building, a shadow outside the glare of the arc lights. It was all so familiar.

Familiar? No, not really.

Joe had seen the Worthington High Tigers on the playing field before, but always as a group of dudes he did not like and did not care about. They were nothing—absolutely nothing—in his life. Now though, he was going to be running against them. He saw them in a different light. He had seen Coach McCarthy plenty of times. The last time they met was late in the spring, near the end of the semester, when the coach had caught Joe smoking a cigarette in the boys' rest room. That meeting cost Joe five days in the early morning detention hall. But now Gibson McCarthy was the

71

opposing coach, sending tacklers out to knock Joe to the ground. Joe had seen the bleachers, the short chain-link fence, old man McCrory, the striped scoreboard—the whole scene—so many times. But always from the other side. No, the scene now was not familiar at all. It was different, really different.

A couple of times Joe thought he spotted Worthington players watching him and commenting to each other. For sure they knew about Joe Atkins, a streak of lightning, a tough runner, a good receiver. Gibson McCarthy would have told them, same as Earl Steel always warned the Wildcats about the dangerous threats in an upcoming opponent's lineup. The Worthington Tigers must know, too, that the Joe Atkins they were being cautioned about was the same Joe Atkins they had ignored at Worthington High. The thought gave Joe great satisfaction. What a jolt it must have been for the snoots on the Worthington High team to find out that ol' Joe Atkins was the player they had to stop if they wanted to win. Yes, it must have come as a real surprise.

Nervously, Joe had scanned the chain-link fence and the bleacher crowd since first taking the field. He was searching for Richard's scowling face and Marty's grinning one. They and the others were bound to be here, leaning on the fence, or sitting in the bleachers, or hanging around under them. Joe did not want to see them. But he could not help looking for them.

"You with us?" Paul's barking voice interrupted Joe's thoughts.

"Huh? Sure," Joe said, breaking into a trot to take his place in the lineup for the next dummy play.

Three plays later, Earl Steel and Steve Howard were out on the field waving the players to the sideline and sending Paul and Cramer onto the field for the coin toss.

Joe stood at the sideline, his helmet dangling from his right hand, his eyes fixed on the figures at the center of the field. He did not look past them to the row of Worthington players facing him from the opposite sideline. He did not glance beyond the Worthington players at the bleachers rising up behind them. Nor did he look backward at the bleachers behind him.

He thought he heard a voice shouting above the crowd noise—"Hey, Joe-baby!"—but the call could have been intended for anyone.

The first quarter was almost half gone. The Worthington Tigers, taking the opening kickoff, had punched their way down the field—short stabs into the line, wide sweeps around the ends, always on the ground—and now stood on the Wildcats' twelve-yard line. In the bleachers the Worthington fans were calling for a touchdown at the top of their voices. Across the field, the Worthington players were standing along the sideline adding their shouts to those of their fans.

The Tigers were proving as tough as Earl Steel had warned. They had been whipped once, but as the coach pointed out, they had bounced back the next week and handed the Meadowcliff Ramblers a worse beating than the Wildcats' 31–7 victory. Now the Tigers were threatening to score and take the lead over the undefeated Graham High Wildcats.

The Wildcats strung out along the sideline were a quiet bunch as they watched the defensive unit on the field move into position. For the last five minutes Earl Steel had paced furiously up and down in front of them, stopping only long enough to send in a substitute with fresh instructions for the defense.

The Worthington players broke their huddle and lined up. The quarterback flapped his arms in a signal to the roaring crowd for silence. He was afraid his own teammates would not be able to hear the snap signal above the din. The shouts died down. The quarterback stepped up to the center and barked his signals. He took the snap, rolled out, and pitched to a flanker coming around. The flanker took in the ball.

The flanker tucked in the ball and ran two steps. Then Dave Horton, crashing through from his linebacker position, slammed into him. Dave stopped the flanker cold in his tracks. He went down—and the ball went up.

For what seemed like a full minute the ball hung in the air, and nobody moved.

Then the ball fell. It hit the ground, took a funny bounce, and landed in front of a startled Dave Horton. Dave was on his knees in the process of getting up from the tackle. He pounced on the ball on the fourteen-yard line.

The stadium was suddenly silent. Then a roar went up from the Wildcats' sideline and from a small group of Graham High fans seated together in the bleachers behind the bench.

Joe put on his helmet and, snapping the chin strap as he went, jogged onto the field with the Wildcats' offense unit. From behind he heard Earl Steel shouting, "Now we go! Now we go!" In front, Joe saw Dave Horton, gleefully leaping and twisting and shooting a fist in the air as he made his way to the sideline. The players around Dave were slapping him on the shoulder pads.

In the huddle, Paul called a play sending Andy churning into the line. The Wildcats' own fourteen-yard line was no place for a dangerous pitchout or the risk of a pass.

Andy took the handoff from Paul, snuggled the ball into his stomach with both hands, and plunged toward the broad back of Cramer Springer blocking in the line. Fighting and thrashing for every inch, Andy gained five yards.

Three more times Andy hit the line—first right, then left, then right again—and Chuck Slater went knifing over tackle for six yards, placing the Wildcats on their own thirty-four-yard line with a first down.

"Okay, Atkins," Paul said in the huddle, nodding in Joe's direction. He called for a quick sideline pass to Joe. Joe nodded.

Lined up, Joe glanced at the defensive halfback opposite him. He did not know him. The halfback was watching Joe closely and shifting his weight nervously from one foot to the other. On the previous plays Joe had alternated between blocking him and luring him to the sideline with a buttonhook pass pattern. This time the defender seemed more anxious. He seemed somehow to know that the play—a pass—was going to Joe. The time had ended for those bone-crushing plunges into the line by Andy Walker and the slanting runs off tackle by Chuck Slater. The time had arrived for the flanker with the good hands and the lightning speed to do his stuff.

Joe looked back over his left shoulder at Andy. He hoped the glance telegraphed a false message to the defensive halfback: Andy was getting the ball again.

Paul took the snap, faked a handoff to Andy, and rolled back a couple of steps with the ball on his hip.

Joe ran straight ahead, toward the defensive back, lowered his left shoulder in a fake to the inside, and cut sharply back to his right toward the sideline. The defensive back took the fake and Joe, heading the other way, left him behind. On the second stride, Joe looked back over his right shoulder. The ball was there. He pulled it in. His momentum carried him out of bounds. It was a seven-yard gain.

"Same play," Paul said in the huddle. He looked at Joe. "You faked that guy right out of his skin. He can be had again. I'll throw a little quicker. Maybe you can stay in bounds."

Again, Joe darted straight toward the defensive

halfback. This time the halfback backpedaled in front of Joe, trying to leave himself enough room to read a fake or, if he got fooled again, time to recover from the fake.

Joe looked left and turned his shoulders. The defender hesitated. He wasn't taking the fake. Then Joe saw him plant his left foot. His body leaned—only slightly, but enough— and Joe knew he was preparing to move to Joe's left. He was taking the fake. Joe cut sharply back to his right. He was alone. He looked back quickly. The ball was coming in. He put up his hands and brought in the ball. He tucked it away and veered sharply back to his left, still a yard inside the boundary. Downfield, he saw only space between himself and the goal. He shifted into high gear. Then something—hard and painful—slammed into his hip from the side and knocked him across the sideline, out of bounds and into a heap on the ground. But he had gained twelve yards on the play, and a first down for the Wildcats on the Worthington forty-seven-yard line.

Andy slapped Joe on the shoulder pads when he returned to the huddle.

"One more?" Paul asked.

Joe frowned at the quarterback. He knew that the first rule of the football huddle stated that nobody argued with the quarterback's call. But Joe said, "They're not going to fall for that one all night long."

"I mean, inside this time."

"Uh-huh. Okay."

Paul called for the quick pass over center to Joe racing along behind the line of scrimmage.

Lining up, Joe almost grinned at the defensive halfback facing him. He was taking on the forlorn look of someone who knows he is being picked on and can't do anything about it.

With the snap, Joe ran four steps toward the halfback. Then, not bothering with a fake to his right, he cut to his left. The beleaguered defensive halfback interpreted Joe's cut as another fake to the left, a prelude to a run to the right. Joe left him behind again.

The ball was there, a dropping rifle shot, almost before Joe made his cut. His arms were out and his hands were reaching. The ball rocketed into his hands. He grabbed and held on.

Out of the corner of his eye, Joe saw the flashing form of a linebacker slamming on the brakes and reversing himself. He also had taken Joe's cut as a fake and had started over to help the defensive halfback. It was a mistake. Now the linebacker was out of the play. Joe was alone.

Joe pulled the ball in and veered to his right, toward the goal.

A blue uniform loomed up into view for a moment, over to Joe's right, dangerously close and moving in. Then it vanished under a flying blur of orange. Somebody, probably Cramer, had cut down the tackler.

Joe was free. He turned on the speed. He thought

he heard the thundering footbeats of a tackler behind him, but the sound faded away as he ran. He crossed the thirty, the twenty, the ten, the goal.

Circling in the end zone he saw Andy, who had followed him down the field, ready to deliver a block if any of the Worthington Tigers had seemed capable of catching Joe. Andy was heading toward him, a wide grin on his face.

Joe tossed the ball to the referee and began jogging toward the bench. At the ten-yard line, Andy met him with a bear hug, lifting him off the ground and swinging him around. Then others—Cramer, Chuck, Charlie Janis, Matthew Jefferies—crowded around him. Joe was grinning when he escaped the crowd and trotted to the bench. The players along the sideline moved out to slap him on the back. Earl Steel squeezed Joe's arm and said, "Nice play," but the coach's eyes were already on the field where the Wildcats were lining up for the try for the extra point.

The bleachers, packed with Worthington fans, were quiet as Ron Sterling's placekick tumbled end over end over the crossbar for the extra point.

Out of the quiet, Joe heard the call—"Hey, Joe-baby!"—and there was no mistaking the voice. And there was no mistaking the Joe who was the object of the call. The voice, high-pitched and laughing, was Marty's.

Joe turned from the field toward the sound of the voice. There seemed to be nothing else to do.

CHAPTER 9

There they were—Marty, Richard, a couple of the others—leaning on the chain-link fence. Any minute now, old man McCrory was sure to spot them and come striding over to chase them back to the bleachers. Joe knew the drill. But for now, there they were.

Joe shifted his helmet from his right hand to his left and gave them a wave. "Hey," he called. "How're you doing?"

Marty was leaning over the short fence, his face thrust forward, giving Joe a leering smile. "Joe-baby," he shouted. "We been reading about you in the papers. You're a big hero now."

Marty had been drinking. Joe had seen the signs plenty of times before.

Next to Marty, Richard stood in a slouch, his hip leaning against the fence, his arms folded across his chest. Richard was not grinning. He was staring at Joe as if he were some strange creature from another planet. Probably Richard had been drinking, too, but with him it was harder to tell. Drunk or sober, Richard looked and acted pretty much the same.

Joe managed a grin at Marty's wisecrack and shrugged his shoulders. Then he turned his attention back to the field where the players were lining up for the Wildcats' kickoff.

"Hey, Joe, c'mere. C'mon over here." Marty's voice seemed to ring out in the quiet of the stadium like an announcement on the public address system. "C'mon and see your ol' buddies."

Joe rolled his eyes toward the skies. Where in the world was old man McCrory? He always had seemed to be pretty quick to chase them away when Joe was among those leaning against the chain-link fence. But where was he now? What was keeping him?

"Are you a snoot now?" Marty shouted.

Joe turned. He felt a flash of anger. This was not fair. He wanted to walk to the fence and punch Marty in the mouth. He glared at Marty and felt his jaw muscles go taut. Richard lit a cigarette and took a deep puff, watching Joe without expression.

Marty's face changed to a mimic of a pout. "Aw, Joe's mad now," he said.

Old man McCrory finally swooped onto the scene.

Joe did not watch the biology teacher hustle them away from the fence. He turned back to the field and stared blankly at the scene: Ron Sterling moving forward for the kickoff, the players in orange beginning their charge forward to tackle the ball carrier, the players in blue grouping in the center to form a blocking wedge for the runner. But it was all a blur to Joe. He stood motionless, barely aware of the collisions taking place in front of him.

"Friends of yours?"

Joe looked to his left and brought Andy's grinning face into focus. Sure, Andy had heard it all. Probably everyone had heard everything.

"Some guys I used to know at Worthington High," Joe said. After a pause, he added, "Just trying to give me a hard time, you know."

Andy turned his attention back to the field, apparently dismissing the episode from his mind.

But beyond Andy, Joe saw Paul King. Paul had been watching old man McCrory shoo Marty and Richard and the others back to the bleachers, and now he was staring at Joe with a frown on his face. Their eyes met for a moment. Joe turned away.

"Yeah, I know, Mr. Snoot," Joe mumbled under his breath. "You made me put out my cigarette at the tennis courts."

"Huh?" Andy asked.

"Nothing," Joe said.

By halftime, the Wildcats held a commanding 21–0 lead. On defense, the Graham High team, led by

Dave Horton from his lineback position, were stopping the Tigers cold every time. And on offense, with Cramer Springer and Charlie Janis clearing the way, Andy and Chuck pounded through for steady gains, each scoring a touchdown. Joe, after catching three straight passes in the first touchdown drive, pulled in two more of Paul King's rifle shots. Two other passes to Joe went incomplete—a misfire that was out of his reach and a pass that he dropped when ball and tackler arrived at the same instant.

Richard and Marty and the others never reappeared. Maybe old man McCrory sent them packing. Joe remembered more than once when the teacher sought out the policeman on duty at the game and had them escorted from the stadium. Joe hoped they were gone. But he could not be sure.

On the field, none of the Worthington players said anything to Joe. He did not get any of the wisecracks he had feared, or even a word of recognition. But they recognized him. There was no doubt about it. He saw it in their eyes. Whenever he caught a pass, he saw them watching him with a funny look. When he was getting to his feet after running tough—fighting, pounding, thrashing, never letting the first tackler bring him down—he saw the funny look in their eyes. Was this the Joe Atkins they had heard about in the corridors of Worthington High last year? Yes, they recognized him.

In the locker room during halftime, Earl Steel and

Steve Howard were moving around, suggesting, criticizing, praising.

"You're going to do a lot of resting in the second half," Earl Steel said to Joe. "You'll just return kicks."

Joe, seated on a bench and slumped back against a locker, nodded at the coach. He understood. With the Wildcats out front by three touchdowns, the second-stringers were going to see most of the action now. Jason McNeal was going to run the flanker patterns.

Joe did not welcome the coach's statement. For sure, he wanted to play. That was the fun of the game. But there was a bigger reason he wanted to be on the field. There, and only there, was he safe from Richard and Marty and the others. Standing on the sideline, or even seated on the bench, he was an easy target for Marty's jibes. Maybe they were gone, and there was no danger of their returning. But old man McCrory could be eluded. Joe knew that for a fact.

"You've played well," Steel said.

"Thanks."

Joe stood back on the fifteen-yard line, arms dangling at his sides, awaiting the kickoff opening the second half. On both sides of the field, players were on their feet along the sideline and people in both bleachers were standing. Ahead of him, Joe saw the backs of his teammates spread across the field, poised to block the onrushing tacklers.

From behind, Joe thought he heard a shriek—

"Hey, Joe-baby!"—and a laugh. Maybe it was his imagination. Maybe not. The shout and the laugh could have been for real—they could have come from somewhere beyond the fence behind the end zone, outside the stadium.

Joe quit wondering about the shout. The ball, tumbling end over end, was coming down out of the arc lights. The players in front of him were moving. Joe heard the sound—*whack!*—of blocker slamming into tackler. He felt the ball in his hands.

He looked up the field as he tucked the ball away. He began running, heading for the right sideline. His teammates were moving in the same direction, setting up a wall of blockers, trying to build a safe corridor for Joe to race through. The Worthington Tigers realized what was happening—this was a sideline run instead of the Wildcats' usual charge up the middle—and began veering their charge in that direction.

Joe crossed the thirty, then the thirty-five, and was at the sideline. He saw the wavy line of blockers in orange jerseys battling to keep out the blue-shirted Worthington tacklers. The play was working. The corridor was open. Joe could see the path in front of him.

Joe turned on his sprinter's speed. He was sixty-five yards from the goal, but he really needed to escape the tacklers for only fifteen or twenty yards. Once across the fifty-yard line, he should have left the last threat behind him.

But he saw sudden trouble as he approached the midfield stripe. A blue shirt burst through the Wildcats' line and lunged into Joe's path. Joe tried to fake the tackler out of position, but the corridor was narrow and Joe had no place to go. The tackler knew it and ignored the fake. Joe put his head down and thundered into the tackler with all the power he had. If the tackler was going to nail him, Joe was determined to extract a high price. Knees pumping high, he crashed into the opposing player. At the moment of impact, his legs still churning, Joe spun. He felt the tackler give ground to the jolt of the collision. He felt the grabbing hands slipping around his hips. Joe kept pumping his legs. He was pulling free. He could feel it. But then another body in a blue jersey slammed into him from the side. The three of them, Joe and the two tacklers, tumbled to the ground out of bounds in front of the Graham High bench.

Steve Howard extended a hand and helped Joe to his feet. "Good job," he said.

Joe nodded. He knew he was going to have another one of those black bruises on his hip. He went to the bench while Jason McNeal entered the game at flanker.

For Joe the game was finished except for punt returns. He sat on the bench, shoulders hunched forward, elbows on knees, watching Jason play the flanker position. He waited for the cry—"Hey, Joe-baby!"—but it never came.

At the finish the scoreboard showed the Graham High Wildcats the victors by a score of 35–0.

Joe felt a sense of relief when finally he stood up, watched the last seconds tick off the scoreboard clock, and trotted to the locker room for his shower.

Joe saw them when he stepped out of the building and headed for the team bus. They were standing in front of the bus, just off to the side, outside the head-lights' beams. A couple of cigarettes glowed in the darkness.

Some of the Graham High players already were on the bus. Others, strung out ahead of Joe, were climbing aboard. A few were still inside, finishing dressing.

Joe slowed to a stop in the darkness. They were waiting for him, and they probably had recognized him in the light as soon as he stepped out the door-way. They were going to poke fun at him, call him a hero and a snoot—or maybe just talk. There was no guessing what they might do or say, and what Andy or Paul or any of the players—or even Earl Steel— might hear.

Joe measured his chances of quickly walking to the bus and stepping aboard before they could approach him. The chances were pretty slim. Besides, if he got on the bus without speaking to them, obviously trying to elude them, he probably would have them facing him at the window.

He thought of returning to the locker room. He

could pretend he had forgotten something. Then he could stall around long enough to walk out with Earl Steel and Steve Howard, who were always the last to leave. If he were walking with the coaches, even Marty might be cowed enough to keep his mouth shut. But no, no. That would be guaranteeing that the coaches saw them and heard whatever they might say.

Keeping his eyes on the bus, away from the shadowy figures behind the glowing cigarettes, Joe walked straight toward the door.

"Hey, Joe." The voice was Richard's.

Joe stopped. "Hey," he said. He unconsciously looked around. Nobody was paying any attention to him. He turned and walked toward them.

"How you doing?" Richard asked.

"Okay."

"You looked pretty good out there—what we saw."

Joe smiled slightly. So old man McCrory had hustled them out of the stadium. A year ago Joe never would have guessed he would have a reason to be thankful to the biology teacher. "A lucky night," he said finally.

"Yeah. You always were lucky."

"Uh-huh."

After a moment's pause, Richard said, "Listen, Marty didn't—I mean, we—didn't mean to embarrass you out there."

"Ah, don't worry about it."

"We'd been reading about you in the papers, and

everything, you know. And then, well, there you were."

"Don't worry about it." Joe spoke the words in an easy conversational tone. This was going better than he could have hoped. "Nothing to worry about."

"Kinda funny, seeing ol' Joe out there on the field being a hero with all those dudes."

Joe glanced beyond Richard at Marty. Richard was doing all the talking. Marty was standing back and staying quiet. Maybe Richard had given him a hard time for shouting at Joe on the sideline, with everyone listening and watching.

"Well," Joe said, "those dudes won't be so high and mighty on Monday, will they, after what we did to them out there tonight."

"That's for sure."

Joe took a deep breath. "Well, gotta go," he said, turning back to the bus.

"Wait a minute."

Joe stopped.

"I've got the car tonight. We can run you back over to Graham."

"Can't do it. Team rule. Everyone has to ride the team bus."

"You didn't use to worry so much about rules."

Joe didn't like the cutting edge to Richard's voice. He didn't want any trouble in front of the players watching from the bus and the players walking by and climbing aboard. "Besides," he said, ignoring

Richard's jibe, "it's a three-hour drive, you know."

Richard shrugged easily. "Nothing else to do," he said.

"I can't. The coaches won't even let us ride home with our parents.'

"What if you just went with us? What are they going to do—come after you?"

"No, I can't do it. Really."

Richard took a drag on his cigarette and flipped it away. "Well, we'll be seeing you over there in Graham one of these weekends," he said. He made the statement sound like a dare.

"Sure. Okay."

"We've talked about it, and we're going to do it." This time it sounded almost like a threat.

"Sure. Okay. See you later."

Joe stepped onto the bus with a deep frown on his face.

Through the bus window he watched Richard gun the car out of the parking lot, tires screeching. When the red taillights disappeared, he put his chin on his fist and stared into the darkness of the bus.

CHAPTER 10

"Hey," Andy said. "Where were you Saturday night?"

Andy and Joe were standing next to each other in front of their lockers, peeling off their street clothes to dress for the Monday practice.

"Saturday night? Home. No, I went to a movie. Why?"

"The party. Why didn't you come to the party?"

"What party?"

"At Paul's house. I thought you'd be there."

Joe stared at Andy, a hundred thoughts racing through his mind. He managed a casual shrug. "Nobody . . . I mean, I didn't know about any party."

"Didn't Paul . . . ?" Andy's voice trailed off to nothing, and the big grin he usually wore was fading away. His face showed that he wished he had not spoken.

"Nobody said anything," Joe said. He looked away from Andy and resumed unbuttoning his shirt. He felt his defenses rising, same as they always had done at Worthington High. He wanted to finish undressing and get into his practice uniform—fast—to get away from Andy. He did not want to talk. Snoots were snoots, no matter where you were. Only difference this time, he told himself, was that the snoots were his teammates. He clamped his teeth tightly and felt his jaw muscles go taut. It was the old feeling from Worthington High. "It doesn't matter," he said. "I'm not much for parties, anyway."

But Andy wasn't ready to end the discussion. He leaned in close. "Didn't somebody say something to you?"

"Nope."

"Everybody was talking about it in the locker room," Andy said. "You must have heard."

In the locker room after the game with Worthington High, Joe's thoughts had been back on the field, with the cry—"Hey, Joe-baby!"—echoing in his head. He had heard the cry while he was showering. He had heard it while he was dressing in front of his locker. Maybe everyone around him was talking about a party at Paul's house. Maybe even somebody mentioned the party to him. But the cry—"Hey, Joe-baby!"—was drowning out everything else in Joe's mind.

"And everybody was talking about it on the bus coming back," Andy added.

But on the bus, too, anyone's words might have sailed past Joe unnoticed. He had made the ride back to Graham slumped in his seat, his chin on his fist, the frown still in place, staring out the window into the darkness. Richard's parting remark—"We'll be seeing you over there in Graham"—refused to leave his mind. The three-hour bus ride back to Graham was a long blur.

Joe had believed everything now was going to be okay. But Worthington High and his problems were going to follow him to Graham. The prospect was horrifying. All he needed was just one bit of trouble—one hint—and he was a goner. Earl Steel was not one to put up with a troublemaker for a minute. Neither were most of the players. Even Andy. Joe did not want to lose what he had won, but he saw Richard and Marty pulling it all out of his hands. How could he stop them? He did not know. If they showed up in Graham, he could not afford to turn his back on them. If they got the idea that Joe had gone snoot on them, they were sure to haunt him forever, just for the fun of it. Joe knew the way their heads worked.

Joe was already finding things difficult with some of the snoots—Paul, Jason, the others. Paul still remembered the episode with the cigarette at the tennis courts, and so did his friends. The evidence of Paul's remembering was in the party at his house, which Joe had not been invited to attend. Snoots knew how to squeeze a guy and keep him in his place, even if the guy did score touchdowns.

"Well," Joe said, "maybe somebody said something about a party, but I never heard it."

"I should have called you on Saturday."

Joe turned and looked at Andy. The brawny fullback was grinning again. Joe figured that not all dudes, not all snoots, were so bad. Andy was a good guy. In fact, he was not a snoot at all. But Joe decided against telling Andy that he had tried to call him on Saturday evening about joining him at the movie and had wondered where Andy had gone without him.

"It wasn't such a hot party, anyway," Andy said.

Joe could not help returning Andy's grin as he finished undressing and reached into his locker for his practice uniform.

Nobody else asked why Joe had missed the party. Nobody at all.

Through the rest of the practice week—Tuesday, Wednesday, Thursday—Joe felt more and more like an outsider when around his teammates.

In the classroom and corridors at school, on the streets around town, he still drew smiles, waves, and friendly hellos. After all, he was Joe Atkins—the pass catcher, the tough runner, the big reason the Graham High Wildcats were undefeated after five games.

But in the locker room and on the practice field, he could not escape the feeling that most of the players were shunning him. There seemed to be fewer calls of "good catch" and "good run" from his teammates.

When he lunged forward and snared a Paul King pass that anyone else would have dropped—or not even reached—he got nothing more than a nod of acknowledgment from the quarterback. When he put a hand on Cramer Springer's back and guided him into a needed block, then scampered twenty-one yards in the Wednesday scrimmage, Cramer said nothing. The players seemed to be standing apart from him, as if they had received a signal from someone about not being friendly with Joe Atkins.

Except Andy. He chattered with Joe at the lockers before and after practice. He sent out his cheers with a grin when Joe grabbed a pass or eluded a tackler. He seemed oblivious to the fact that the others were ignoring his friend.

"These guys are doing a number on me," Joe said to Andy when they were walking through the corridor following Thursday's final class, heading for the locker room to dress for practice.

"Ah, it's your imagination."

"No, it's not."

"Well, don't worry about it. You worry too much."

Andy seemed never to worry about anything. He ran with the power of an eighteen-wheeler tractor-trailer rig, and seemed sure that was all that mattered. He never cared what anyone thought, even about him buddying around with Joe Atkins.

"I just don't get it," Joe said.

"You're new, that's all."

"I'm not *that* new."

For a moment they walked along without speaking. Briefly, Joe regretted opening up to Andy. He had learned a long time ago not to admit that someone was putting him down. That was the same as admitting that it mattered. And admitting that it mattered was, well, a sign of weakness. Tough guys, he knew, never gave off signs of weakness.

"Look," Andy said slowly, "a lot of the guys on the team kind of look to Paul, you know. He's a senior, the quarterback, and the captain." Andy shrugged his shoulders slightly. "And he goes strictly by the rules, if you know what I mean."

Joe nodded. He knew, all right.

"Paul spotted you with a cigarette at the tennis courts, and told you it's against regulations to smoke on the school grounds."

Joe's right eyebrow went up. So Paul *had* spread the word around. All he said was, "Uh-huh."

Andy, as if reading Joe's mind, said, "Yeah, he told Coach Steel, too."

"Nice," Joe said.

"But what's it matter?" Andy asked, leaning in close. "Coach Steel's got you in the starting lineup. He wouldn't be doing that, believe me, if he thought anything was wrong with you."

Joe waited.

"Paul always likes to tell people they're doing something wrong because he never does. You've just got to understand that that's Paul."

"Yeah, I know the type."

"Well, then, when those guys at Worthington were hollering at you—it was pretty obvious, you know, that the loud one was drunk—and they were your old buddies, and—"

"But I don't see what any of this has to do with anything."

"Nothing, really, I guess. But—"

"But what?"

"Look, I don't want to make things any worse."

"I want to know what's going on. So I smoked a cigarette one day before I even thought of coming out for football. What's the big deal? It's not like I've been lighting up in the locker room or in the huddle. And so a couple of guys I knew back at Worthington High shouted at me. So what does it matter? What do they have to do with anything? *I'm* the one who's catching passes. *I'm* the one who's running for yardage."

They stopped at the end of the corridor, now almost empty of students. Joe was breathing heavily. Again he regretted what he had said. He was revealing himself to Andy, and Joe Atkins never revealed himself. He was asking how he could win approval, and tough guys never asked for approval. Tough guys laughed at approval. Joe wanted to turn and walk away—from Andy, from the football team, from Graham High. But he stayed where he was.

"Paul's so straight-arrow, and—"

"I understood what you meant already."

—"and a lot of the players, well, they look up to him, and—"

"You said that before, too."

Andy took a deep breath. "I think Paul figures you might let the team down. That you might get into some kind of trouble or something, and not be there when we need you. That you might do something to get yourself bounced off the team, or even expelled. I think Paul feels that we shouldn't be counting on you too much." He paused. "Do you see what I mean?"

"Yeah, but it's stupid."

Andy grinned at him. "Sure, it's stupid—and that's why I told you in the first place to forget it. Don't pay any attention. And don't let your imagination run away with you."

Joe stared at Andy for a moment, his jaw tightly clenched. Then he said softly, "Uh-huh."

"C'mon, we're going to be late," Andy said. Then, still grinning, he added, "Paul will be saying, 'See, I told you so, and the guy has taken Andy Walker off with him.' I've got a reputation to maintain."

Joe followed Andy around the turn in the corridor and down the steps leading to the locker room.

He was not smiling.

For Joe, practice was a disaster. He dropped passes. He ran his patterns wrong—a step too short, a step too far, a cut the wrong way. Once, he turned and ran the wrong way in the backfield, colliding with Paul and

Chuck at the instant of the handoff, busting the play. And at every turn, whether he ran the play the right way or the wrong way, he saw everyone's face, even Andy's, turned toward him. And he was sure they were all thinking the same thing. Joe Atkins did not fit in. Joe Atkins did not belong. He belonged on the other side of the fence, with the guy who had been drinking at Worthington. He was Joe Atkins's friend. Joe Atkins belonged over there, over the fence, with his friend.

Earl Steel finally called Joe aside. "What's wrong?" he asked.

"Nothing."

Steel stared at him with those icy blue eyes.

"Nothing," Joe repeated.

"Your mind is a million miles away. Are you sure . . . ?"

"Sure."

Finally practice ended. Joe jogged in from the field and quickly removed his practice uniform, finished his shower, got dressed, and left for home.

And that night, for the first time since school opened, Joe went to bed without studying.

What difference did it make?

CHAPTER 11

By game time on Friday night, Joe had spent a lot of time trying to convince people—his parents, Coach Earl Steel, himself—that nothing was wrong.

His parents had been quick to spot his change in mood. "No, no, no, nothing's wrong," he had told them at the breakfast table. Maybe they believed him. Maybe not. Either way, they laid off. Probably they thought he was nervous about the game.

He had convinced Earl Steel—maybe—when the coach stopped him in the corridor between classes. Steel asked again, "Is anything wrong?" Joe answered again, "No, nothing." Steel glared at him a moment, then walked on.

Joe had convinced himself of several things. First, he had decided it would not do any good to punch Paul King in his goody-goody face, although he wanted to do it. Second, he was not going to quit the football team. He was not about to let a bunch of snoots run him off. And third, he was going to go back to his feelings on that first day of practice—he was again going to be like that newcomer, that outsider, who mixed with the dudes and heroes but didn't care what they thought, because playing football was all that really mattered.

The one person who required no convincing was Andy Walker. Andy, with his smile in place, seemed in full agreement with Joe's repeated protestations— "No, no, nothing is wrong." Somehow, Joe found Andy's unflagging faith more difficult to understand than the probing questions of his parents, the recurring inquiries of Earl Steel, and his own uncertainties. How could Andy be so sure? Maybe Andy simply did not understand.

Under the bright glare of the arc lights, Joe stretched and bent through the pre-game calisthenics. He ran out for passes. He moved down the field in the signal drill. And through it all, Joe either glanced at his teammates as if they were strangers or did not look at them at all. He refused to wonder if they were watching him or to guess at their thoughts. He simply ignored them. He said nothing and he heard nothing beyond Paul's barking of the signals.

At one point he spotted Earl Steel watching him. "Don't worry," he murmured under his breath to himself as if replying to the coach's unasked question.

"I've got it all figured out now. This won't be like the Thursday afternoon practice. My mind is here—right here on the football field—and not wandering around a million miles away."

In fact, Joe felt an intensity—a degree of concentration—greater than any he had felt in previous games.

Earl Steel and Steve Howard were waving the players to the sideline for the final moments before the start of the game.

Joe, walking toward the bench, glanced across the field. The Woodruff Bears, in their white uniforms with red trim, were moving toward their coach at the sideline. There was nothing scary about them. They had lost three of their five games. They lacked offensive punch and their defense was slow and weak. They were not going to be much of a test for the Wildcats. Even Earl Steel had seemed calm and confident during the week.

The bleachers on both sides of the field were packed, and an overflow of fans lined the fences on both sides. The Graham High fans, with their team undefeated, were already tasting the Wildcats' first championship in years.

From the rumbling crowd noise, Joe occasionally heard his name—"Get 'em, Atkins!" and, "All the way, Joe!"—with each shout ending in a roar from the fans.

Once, when his name rang out above the noise,

Joe's eyes met Paul King's. Paul might have given Joe a thumbs-up sign. Or maybe a thumb-and-fore-finger circle to signal that everything was great. Or at least a smile. But instead, nothing. Just a stare. Maybe Paul King, the quarterback, the celebrated passer, did not like having someone crowd into the spotlight with him. Snoots were like that, Joe figured. He looked away from Paul.

Then Paul, along with Cramer Springer, walked to the center of the field for the coin toss. The coin went into the air, and one of the Woodruff captains called it. He was right. The Bears wanted to receive the opening kickoff.

With Paul and Cramer returning to the sideline, Joe moved into the crowd of players encircling Earl Steel. Everybody was shouting and jumping and pummeling each other. Joe did not feel like shouting and jumping and pummeling someone. So he just stood there, staring into space.

The Wildcats' kickoff team took the field, and Joe and the other players strung out along the sideline to watch.

Unconsciously, Joe glanced down at his uniform—bright orange with black trim, and at the helmet in his right hand, bright orange with the black silhouette of a clawing wildcat on each side—and for the millionth time in recent weeks mumbled to himself, "Weird, really weird. Joe Atkins standing out here with the dudes and the heroes, wearing a uniform." He had to admit that Paul King was not the only one who wondered whether Joe Atkins fit in with the Graham High football team.

Joe's first chance to get his hands on the ball was quick in coming. With Dave Horton leading the Graham tacklers in slashing through the hapless Woodruff blockers, the Wildcats stopped their opponents deep in their own territory. After three downs, the Bears had gained a total of four yards, and their punting team moved onto the field. The punter took up his position on the five-yard line.

Joe jogged onto the field and stood at the forty-five-yard line, staring down the field and waiting.

Earl Steel shouted instructions from the sideline.

Joe nodded and moved up to the forty-yard line. Earl Steel probably knew how far the Woodruff punter could kick the ball.

Leaning forward slightly, his arms dangling loosely at his sides, Joe felt his legs go tense when the Woodruff center snapped the ball. Joe watched. The punter got the kick away. It was a low spiral and—Earl Steel had been right—it was short.

Joe sprang forward, taking off after the ball. Now it was falling fast, like a spent rifle shot. Joe knew what a low kick meant: good news for him, bad news for the Woodruff Bears. The onrushing tacklers had less time to reach him, while he had more time to catch the ball, to take the measure of the field in front of him, and to run.

But first he had to catch the ball. He was lunging forward, arms outstretched, fingers reaching, and the ball was falling. There was no question of letting up and allowing the ball to hit the ground, then trying to grab it on the bounce. Too many crazy things happened when a football started bouncing around on the ground. The cardinal rule was simple: always catch the ball in the air.

Joe felt the falling ball hit his fingertips. He was hurtling forward and almost lost his balance. Then he regained it. He had barely made it to the ball. Instinctively, he flicked it upward with his fingertips. He kept running, juggling the ball in front of him. Finally he grabbed it and tucked it away.

At last he was able to take his eyes off the ball and look downfield for the first time. The world in front of him was a wall of white uniforms with red trim, a crowd of Woodruff players. He was racing on a collision course with half the Woodruff team.

He cut sharply to his right, toward the sideline, away from the mass of white uniforms. The blur of an orange uniform flew into the crowd of white ones. Somebody had delivered a powerful block. Joe veered his route downfield, pointing toward the goal. He saw the chalk stripes disappearing beneath him as he ran.

White uniforms flashed by as he ran. He saw them out of the corner of his eye, but none of them got close.

He crossed the goal line without being touched.

He circled in the end zone, tossed the ball to the referee, and jogged back toward the bench.

The roar of the crowd rolled down out of the bleachers onto the field from both sides. He heard his name—*"Atkins! Atkins! Atkins!"*

Andy grabbed Joe in a bear hug and swung him around, grinning. Joe grinned back at him. Cramer met him with a hug, which surprised Joe. At the sideline, players stood waiting for him with their hands out. Joe slapped the hands as he trotted by. One of the hands was Paul King's.

"Nice bit of running," Earl Steel said, patting Joe on the behind.

Joe, puffing, nodded and went to the bench.

Three minutes later, following a Woodruff fumble and the Wildcats' recovery, Joe was back on the field. Paul King sent Andy pounding through the center of the line for eight yards to the eighteen-yard line and then pitched out to Chuck Slater for four yards around end.

In the huddle, Paul glanced at Joe and called the play sending Joe into the end zone in a buttonhook pattern for a pass.

Paul's pass hit the mark and Joe held on—touchdown.

Joe scored twice more before the halftime intermission, first on a short pass from Paul over center and a weaving run through the Woodruff secondary twenty-one yards to the goal, and later on a long pass that came over Joe's shoulder and fell into his hands as he crossed the goal.

Andy scored once on a short plunge and Paul got a touchdown on a keeper.

As he trudged to the locker room at halftime, Joe knew that with the score 42–0, he was through for the night, except for kick returns. The Wildcats' substitutes were sure to play the entire second half.

At the finish the score was 56–7, and the Wildcats' locker room erupted into a wild melee of shouting, cheering, whistling, and laughing. Wet towels flew across the room. Roars of laughter followed each successful shot.

"Cut it," Earl Steel said. He spoke in a conversational tone. But somehow everyone heard his words above the roar of their own noise. The towels stopped flying. The shouting died away. "Try to act like winning is not something new to you," he said, and stalked out of the locker room to the coaches' office down the corridor. The shouting and towel-throwing resumed under the disapproving glare of Steve Howard.

Joe, next to Andy, found himself grinning at the victory party going on around him. He even shouted once, at nobody in particular. After all, he had scored four touchdowns. But then his grin began to fade, and he did not consider shouting again. It would have felt funny. He was not included in the celebration. Nobody had thrown a towel at Joe Atkins. Nobody was shouting at him. The four touchdowns did not matter. He was not a part of that celebration.

Quickly removing his game uniform and pads, he left Andy's side and walked to the showers. He was the first one in. He turned on the water, grabbed a bar of soap, and began to lather. The gushing water drowned out the noise from the locker room except for someone's occasional high-pitched shriek. He was still alone in the shower when he rinsed and turned off the water. He picked a towel off the stack, wrapped it around his waist, and walked back to his locker. The shouting and the cheering were dying down, and nobody was throwing towels. Most of the players were stripping off their uniforms, and some were heading for the showers.

He dried himself quickly and began dressing. Andy was in the shower. Joe particularly wanted to finish dressing and leave before Andy returned. What if Andy invited him to a party somewhere? What would he say?

He buttoned his shirt, stepped into his jeans, and buckled his belt. He did not take the time to comb his hair. He sat down and pulled on his socks and stepped into his shoes. He closed his locker, slammed the lock shut, and twirled the dial of the combination lock.

Joe looked around. Andy still was not in sight. He could hear the shouts of some of the players from the showers. Andy must be among them.

"Great game," somebody said from behind Joe.

Joe turned. It was Cramer Springer, dripping wet with a towel held around his waist.

"Thanks," Joe said, then he turned and walked out of the locker room.

Once in the corridor, he went the long way around to avoid passing the open door of the coaches' office. He did not need another of Earl Steel's questions: "Is anything wrong?" Or another of his complimentary remarks: "Nice game." All he needed was to get out.

He pushed open the heavy door leading out to the parking lot. The arc lights of the playing field in the distance had been turned down. The scoreboard was dark. A dim haze hung over the field in the October night. A few cars waited in the parking lot between the building and the playing field—friends or parents ready to take the players somewhere. Maybe to a party, Joe thought with a snort. He paid no attention to the cars. His own parents, he knew, had gone home after the game. He had only a short walk.

Joe headed toward the street. The headlights of one of the cars blinked on and caught him in the beam. He turned and squinted into the light.

Joe knew who it was even before the door opened on the driver's side and Richard—recognizable in the dim reflection—stepped out.

CHAPTER 12

"Hey, hero," Richard said.

"Hey." Joe walked toward the car.

"We thought we'd come over and visit our old buddy." Richard paused. "But about the time you were scoring your fourth touchdown and everybody was screaming your name, we figured you had become one of the dudes and would be going out with them after the game."

The statement was almost a question, and Joe understood what Richard was asking. Why are you all alone, hero? Why aren't you with a bunch of snoots from the football team? Why aren't you going off to some fancy party with them?

"Me?" Joe said. "Nah, not me. After the game, the snoots go their way and I go mine."

"Well, let's go."

"Sure."

Behind him, the door opened again, letting out a beam of light. Several players walked out amid sounds of laughter. One of them was Paul. Another was Jason. Joe got into the back seat of the car, probably before they had a chance to spot him.

Richard turned the key in the ignition, gunned the engine, slipped the car into gear, and roared across the parking lot. At the street, he cut the wheels sharply and stomped down on the accelerator, sending the rear wheels skidding around with a piercing screech. The car shot down the darkened street.

From the passenger seat in front, Marty turned with a grin and held aloft a vodka bottle. "Want a shot, Joe-baby?"

"Uh, not right now."

"Where we going?" Richard asked.

'What do you want?"

"Action. Where's the action?"

"Okay," Joe said. "Just keep going straight on this street until I tell you to turn." Joe knew the place—the Purple People Eater, a drive-in diner on the edge of town. He never had been there, but he had seen the place and had heard about it. Some of the guys at school hung out there on weekend nights.

"We need some ice and some paper cups," Marty announced from the front seat. "I should've kept the cup I had at the game."

Joe said nothing.

"Hey," Marty said suddenly, turning in the seat to face Joe. "We met the Graham High version of old man McCrory." He giggled. "I guess every school's got one."

"Yeah," Richard said. "He asked if we were from Woodruff." He laughed. "We told him, sure, sure we were."

Joe frowned. He wondered which of the Graham High teachers had the assignment to prowl the bleachers with an eye out for troublemakers. He never had thought of it before. He was always on the other side of the fence, on the field, playing the game. The faculty monitor in the bleachers never concerned him. He hoped that the man who questioned Richard and Marty was not Mr. Bagley, his English teacher. Mr. Bagley was okay. Or Mr. Greene, the social sciences teacher. He was okay, too. What if Richard and Marty had told the teacher that Joe Atkins was their ol' buddy from Worthington High?

"Funny little guy," Marty said. "All bald-headed and everything, you know, and with wire-rim glasses. He got all flustered and didn't seem to know what to say when we told him that we were from Woodruff." Marty giggled. "He couldn't throw out a visiting fan, now could he?"

Joe's frown deepened. It was Mr. Bagley. At least they hadn't told him they were friends of Joe Atkins.

"Turn right at the next stop sign," Joe said. "Then straight for a couple of miles out to the edge of town.

It's on the right—the Purple People Eater. Big purple neon sign."

Marty extended the bottle to Richard. "Huh?" he asked.

"Sure." Richard took the bottle, lifted it to his lips, and tilted it. "Ah," he said, handing the bottle back to Marty.

Marty took a swallow. "Purple People Eater, huh?" he said. Then he laughed. "Is that something purple that eats people? Or is it something that just eats people who are purple?" He laughed again.

"One of life's great mysteries, huh?" Richard said.

The car was racing along the straight blacktop road through the darkness.

Marty extended his left hand over the seat, holding out the bottle to Joe. "Huh?" he asked.

"Why not?" Joe leaned forward and took the bottle. He swallowed a small sip and handed it back to Marty. The vodka felt warm going down and warm in his stomach. "Got a cigarette?" he asked.

Richard extended a pack of cigarettes over his right shoulder while steering with his left hand.

Joe took the pack. "Got a match?" he asked.

Marty handed Joe a book of matches.

Joe struck a match and lit the cigarette. He took a long drag and blew the smoke out. The smoke scratched his throat and he almost coughed. It had been a long time. Not since that day at the tennis courts when goody-goody Paul King had leaped up out of nowhere, all tanned and blond in white tennis uniform, and announced that smoking was against the rules. Who cared about Paul King, anyway? Joe leaned back and took another drag on the cigarette. It wasn't so bad the second time. The vodka still felt warm in his stomach.

Richard slowed the car and turned off the road. Ahead was a huge purple neon sign with a grinning creature—sort of like a frog—peering over the row of letters that spelled out Purple People Eater.

"So that's what a purple people eater looks like," Marty said.

"Now you know," Joe replied from the back seat. It felt good to be with friends again. Nobody in Graham, not even Andy, was a friend he could just hang out with. Sure, he and Andy had done things like going to movies together. Matthew Jefferies and Charlie Janis sometimes went with them. But none of them, not even Andy, was the good-buddy kind of guy who just hung around. This felt good, being with friends, after all this time. "Yep," Joe added, "now you know what a purple people eater looks like."

Richard stopped the car in the middle of the parking lot and looked around. Most of the parking places around the edge of the lot were occupied. Everybody seemed to be out of their car—and outside the cafe, too—roaming around the parking lot, visiting with each other.

"There's a spot," Marty said.

"Where?"

"There." Marty pointed.

Richard pulled the car forward and turned to his right, nosing toward the parking place. A couple of people absently walked in front of the car. Richard gave them a blast of the horn. They jumped. Marty guffawed. Richard said nothing. He edged the car into the parking place.

"Do they come out to your car for your order?" Richard asked.

"I don't know," Joe said. "I've never been here before."

Richard turned in the seat and looked at him. "Really? This looks like where it's at, okay."

Joe shrugged. "Naw, I've never been here." Then he grinned at Richard. "You know how it is with football heroes—early to bed and early to rise."

Richard did not return the grin. "No, I don't know how it is with football heroes." He turned to Marty. "Let's go in and get some stuff. I could use a hamburger. Football games always make me hungry."

"I need some ice and a cup," Marty said. "Football games always make me thirsty."

The doors opened on both sides and Richard and Marty tumbled out of the car. Joe got out on Marty's side.

"What does football make you?" Marty asked Joe. "Hungry or thirsty or both?"

"Football doesn't make me much of anything," Joe

said. He thought about what he had just said and remembered the sound of his own name—*"Atkins!"*—being shouted from the bleachers. He remembered the bear hugs and handslaps from his teammates after a touchdown. He liked those memories. But he remembered other things, too. Like the sinking feeling when Andy asked, "Hey, where were you Saturday night?" And the look on Andy's face when he tried to explain why Paul and the others were keeping their distance. He remembered Paul's face at the Worthington game when Marty was hanging on the fence and shrieking, "Hey, Joe-baby!" Joe did not like those memories.

The three of them walked across the parking lot toward the front door of the Purple People Eater. People were milling around all over the place. Joe spotted some people he recognized, some from the classroom, some from the corridors of Graham High. He returned their nods. He did not see any of the football players.

From his left he heard his name. "Well, well, if it isn't Joe Atkins," the voice said.

Joe turned, and stared into the smiling face of the boy with the locker next to his at school. The boy was holding a paper cup in one hand and a cigarette in the other. He took a drag on the cigarette. He was standing easy, relaxed, watching Joe. He looked confident, almost cocky, in sharp contrast to the uncertain, shrinking-away image he conveyed in the corridor at

Graham High. Joe knew the reason for the difference. Here the boy was on his own turf, with his own kind. He felt comfortable.

The sight of the boy startled Joe, same as it had in front of the lockers. Joe again had the eerie feeling that he was looking at himself back at Worthington High.

"Hi," Joe said. "How're you doing?"

"I'm doing fine, just fine."

Joe nodded and turned to catch up with Richard and Marty.

Inside, they ordered hamburgers and soft drinks, paid the bill, and stepped back outside onto the parking lot.

Marty headed for the car where he had left the vodka bottle stashed under the front seat. Richard and Joe followed him. They gathered around the passenger side of the car, their food and cups on the hood, while Marty fished around under the seat for the bottle.

"It's gone!" Marty shouted from inside the car. He withdrew from the car and stood up, a mixed expression of genuine alarm and genuine anger on his face. "Somebody's swiped our vodka."

"Aw, c'mon, it's not gone," Joe said.

Richard said nothing. He already was scanning the milling crowd of people, looking for someone holding a vodka bottle.

"Uh-oh," Joe said aloud. Trouble was cooking. Big

trouble. He had seen it before. He had been in the middle of it before. Somebody accused somebody of something. Somebody denied it. Somebody took offense. Then somebody took a swing, and somebody else took a swing. Suddenly, it was too late to stop things and they got out of hand in a big way, fast. In the end nobody could remember who started it, or even why it started. But it had started. Joe had seen it many times.

Joe dived toward the front floorboard and thrust his hand deep under the seat. Nothing. He came out of the car and straightened up. Richard was walking away, and beyond him, Joe saw somebody with a vodka bottle in his hand. Marty was a couple of steps behind Richard.

Joe went back into the car, leaned over the seat, and peered at the floor of the back seat. There it was. The bottle had rolled out from under the front seat when Marty shoved it under.

Joe came back out of the car. "Hey! Here it is!" he shouted. "I found it."

Richard was six feet from the somebody with a vodka bottle in his hand. He turned. "You found it?"

"Yeah."

Richard took a couple of steps back toward Joe. Then he turned back to the somebody and said, "You don't know how lucky you are."

Joe saw the somebody look around at Richard with an expression of puzzlement. Then, almost instantly, the expression turned to one of hostility and Joe heard him say, "Huh? What did you say?"

"C'mon," Joe shouted.

Richard stared silently at the somebody for a moment, and then turned and walked back to the car, with Marty trailing behind him.

Joe handed the bottle to Marty. Marty sloshed vodka into his paper cup.

"Want some?" Marty asked.

"Not right now," Joe said, taking a bite of his hamburger.

Richard took the bottle from Marty without a word and poured into his paper cup. "That guy over there was looking for trouble, and he almost found it," he said.

Joe barely heard the words. He was watching the crowd roaming around the parking lot, some shouting and laughing, some speaking in low tones, some waving at friends across the lot. Some were people he recognized. None were football players. Suddenly everyone looked alike to Joe—identical to the boy with the locker next to his and, somehow, identical to Joe's own face back at Worthington High. Joe blinked and everyone returned to normal.

Joe finished the hamburger. "Gotta go," he said abruptly.

"Go?" Marty stared in disbelief. "We just got here."

"It's getting late."

119

"Late? It's just a little after ten o'clock."

"Yeah, but I'm tired." He tried to put on an easy smile. "If you had had those dudes pounding on you all night out there on the field like I did, you'd be tired, too."

"Tired." Marty mouthed the word as if it were some foreign expression he was trying to speak for the first time.

Richard watched Joe without speaking. He seemed—or at least Joe thought he seemed—to understand what was happening. "Okay," he said. "We'll drive you home."

"Leave? We just got here," Marty repeated.

"No, no," Joe said. "I can walk. I live just over there, not far at all. You guys stay here. No need for you to pull out just because I've got to go." He paused. "Besides, you'd better not give up your parking place. You'd never get another one."

Joe turned and left.

Joe did not live "just over there." He lived two, maybe three, miles away. He knew the direction—back down the same road they had driven to reach the Purple People Eater, and then a turn to the left, back toward the school.

Once away from the parking lot, he cut across the darkened street to the left side so he would be facing the oncoming cars and began jogging. The warm feeling of the vodka was gone from his stomach now.

That was good. But he seemed short of breath all of a sudden. Could one cigarette do that much damage? Could it undo the weeks of strenuous training? Maybe so. Well, the jog home was sure to work it out. That was good.

Occasionally, a car came at Joe on the road. He veered off the road and onto the shoulder. Then when the car's headlights shot by, Joe swerved back onto the edge of the road.

As he jogged, faces kept appearing before him in the darkness—Earl Steel, with his icy stare of disapproval; Andy Walker, with a questioning look; Paul King, with a snooty I-told-you-so expression, all full of self-satisfaction; his own parents, frowning with worry, recalling the problems at Worthington High.

Joe made the turn onto the street where the school was located and jogged on. When he finally passed the school, he knew he was only a few blocks from home. He was no longer short of breath. He felt as if he could run all night. That was good.

It was almost eleven o'clock when he trotted across his front yard, up the steps, and walked across the porch and opened the door.

His father and mother were watching a late movie on television. Joe got a glimpse of John Wayne, wearing a large cowboy hat, saying something to a dark-haired woman who looked scared half to death.

"You're late," his father said.

Joe glanced at his father, and then smiled.

"Did I say something funny?"

Six months earlier, the simple two-word statement from his father would have touched off an argument. The statement would have been an accusation, and Joe, on the defensive, would have thrashed back. "No," he said, "you didn't say anything funny. I was thinking of something else."

"We were beginning to wonder."

"I went out and got a hamburger with some guys."

"Well, I think you were entitled to some celebration. Four touchdowns—pretty spectacular."

"Yeah," Joe said. He managed a slight smile when he imagined his father leaping to his feet in the bleachers with everyone else when Joe crossed the goal line. "I think I'll hit the sack."

"Good night," his father said.

"Sleep well," his mother said.

Inside his room, Joe closed the door. He took a deep breath and exhaled.

"I almost blew it," he said aloud.

CHAPTER 13

The break-in at Graham High was not discovered until Monday morning.

First, the custodian, Mr. Hodges, opening up the building for the day's classes, saw the spray-painted streaks of red on the walls of the corridor in front of the principal's office on the main floor. Then Miss Grayson, the principal's secretary, arrived and opened the door to the principal's office. She took a step backward in shock at the scene before her. File folders and papers were scattered everywhere—on the floor, on desk tops, on tables. The glass top of the conference table was smashed by a swivel chair which now was resting on top of it. Chairs were overturned. Drawers were hanging open in file cabinets. Desk drawers were pulled out and their contents dumped out on the floor. The petty cash box was crushed and empty. The principal, Mr. Crain, came in behind Miss Grayson. He found the broken window in the faculty lounge next to the principal's office. That was how the vandals got into the building.

Joe heard the news about the break-in the moment he walked through the front door of the school. The lobby was packed with students, and everyone was talking about it. The spray-painted streaks were there for everyone to see. The accounts of the damage inside Mr. Crain's office and the faculty lounge were zipping along the student grapevine with record speed.

Everyone was asking the question: "Who did it?"

And they were answering with another question: "Who knows?"

Then someone suggested that the color of the spray-painted streaks—red—offered a clue. The Woodruff High Bears, visitors at the Graham High stadium on Friday night, wore the colors red and white. Maybe someone in from Woodruff for the game had done the damage. Maybe not. The color red may have been nothing more than a coincidence. Or perhaps it was a false clue designed to point investigators in the direction of Woodruff High while the guilty parties really were in Graham.

Or someplace else—like Worthington, perhaps?

The thought hit Joe like a splash of cold water.

He pictured again his last glimpse of Richard and Marty as he walked away from the diner. They were standing alongside Richard's car in the parking lot. They were drinking vodka mixed with cola from their paper cups. They were smoking cigarettes. They were ready for trouble. Joe had seen the signs plenty of times, and he had experienced the results of them.

Joe remembered the night that he and Richard and Marty spray-painted a wall of Mr. Bennett's hardware store. The sudden arrival of a police car caught them by surprise. Joe got away, thanks only to his speed as a runner. Richard and Marty got caught. The color of the spray paint that night had been black. This time it was red.

Joe tried to wipe the thoughts of Richard and Marty from his mind. Milling around with the others in the front lobby before the bell for the first class, Joe hoped his face wasn't giving him away. But he could not rid himself of his thoughts.

He went back in his mind over the brief period he was with them—standing with Richard next to the car in the school parking lot, the ride to the Purple People Eater, the time inside the diner, and then outside in the parking lot. He tried to remember whether any-thing—a remark, or an unidentified object in a paper bag, or something spotted but barely noticed—indi-cated that Richard and Marty had a spray-paint can with them in the darkened car. He could remember nothing. He felt a sense of relief, until he realized that they might have had it in the dashboard compart-ment, or under the driver's seat—anywhere. There were plenty of places they could have kept it. Joe frowned. But if they had had a can of spray paint with them, why didn't they say something to him about it? For sure Marty would have piped up. So why didn't he? Because they didn't have a spray-paint can with them, that's why. Joe managed to return to his sense of relief.

The reports about the smashed petty cash box and the missing money helped ease Joe's mind. In all their ramblings in Worthington, the three of them never went in for thievery. They did not steal money or anything else. Well, maybe once—the time they grabbed a fire extinguisher off the wall at the Voyager Motel. But that wasn't really thievery. They just took the extinguisher to spray some parked cars. No, Richard and Marty might spray-paint a wall, with Marty laughing all the while, but they were not about to steal money.

Coming out of his opening class of the morning, Mr. Bagley's English course, Joe walked through the lobby and saw the police car parked in front of the school. There was something scary about the sight of the car—white and blue with black lettering on the sides and the rack on top holding the twin lights that flashed red during a chase. The car was clear evidence that what had happened at Graham High was serious business. This was no harmless prank, no practical joke. This was severe damage, and thievery.

Through the door to Mr. Crain's office, Joe saw a

uniformed officer talking with Mr. Crain. Another man, wearing a sports jacket and slacks, was with them. Joe figured he probably was a detective.

In the cafeteria during the lunch period, Joe came out of the line with his tray and spotted Andy sitting at a long table with a group of football players. He headed for them and put his tray down next to Andy's tray. As he was seating himself, he caught just the end of something Paul was saying.

". . . for questioning."

"What's that?" Joe asked. "Have they got somebody they're questioning?"

"They're just pulling in some guys for questioning in Mr. Crain's office," Andy said. "I doubt that they've got anything definite on anyone yet."

"Who have they pulled in?"

Paul answered. "The usual bunch—Louie Simpson, Henry Gibson—that bunch, you know."

Joe did not know Louie Simpson or Henry Gibson. But he knew exactly what Paul meant by "that bunch." He knew the type. They were the acknowledged troublemakers of Graham High who always were in the early morning detention hall for skipping classes, smoking pot, keeping a vodka bottle in a locker—the whole array of offenses that Joe knew so well. More than once Joe had found himself seated in the principal's office at Worthington High to answer for something he knew nothing about. When trouble occurred there, Joe's name automatically went on the list of those to be interviewed. And here at Graham High, it was Louie Simpson and Henry what's-his-name and a few others.

"I don't think I know them," Joe said.

"You're better off not knowing them," Paul said.

"Yeah," Andy said with a grin. "They make so much trouble that if you get too close to them, some of it's sure to splash on you."

Joe grinned. He knew what Andy meant.

As he ate, he wondered if the boy with the locker next to his—the boy he had encountered at the Purple People Eater—was Louie Simpson or Henry what's-his-name. If not, he was one of the others whom Paul and Andy were talking about. He would have bet that the boy's name, whatever it might be, was high on Mr. Crain's list.

Joe felt good knowing that for the first time in recent memory his name was not on a list of trouble-makers being drawn up for questioning.

In the first class after lunch, Mrs. Wilde's American History course, Joe sat in the front row and tried to concentrate on the significance of Andrew Jackson's election to the presidency. He almost always drew the front seat because most of the teachers liked to seat the students in alphabetical order. Atkins lost out only to an occasional Abbott or Anderson. At Worthington High, he always squirmed in discomfort in the front row. It was bad news being right under the teacher's nose. But the new Joe Atkins had no problem with a front-row seat. He was not trying to make trouble, and he usually knew the answer when the teacher called on him. It was okay being in the front row—and really okay today, knowing he was not on the principal's list, and also that nobody was concerned about a couple of boys from Worthington High who were in Graham on Friday night.

The classroom door opened and a girl Joe did not know came in, stopping Mrs. Wilde is midsentence. She walked to the teacher's desk and laid a note in front of her.

Mrs. Wilde looked at the girl, then adjusted her glasses and looked down at the note. She looked up at the class and her eyes fell on Joe.

"Joe, you're wanted in the principal's office," she said.

CHAPTER 14

Joe blinked in surprise. He looked at Mrs. Wilde. He looked at the girl waiting impassively next to her desk. His heart suddenly began pounding furiously, and he felt his hands shake slightly. He knew all the eyes in the room were on him.

"Me?" he asked, and then felt stupid for piping up.

"Yes," Mrs. Wilde said. "I'll excuse you to go now."

Joe got to his feet and followed the girl out of the classroom. His head was swimming as he stepped into the corridor. A million questions raced through his mind. Why me? Do they know about me from Worthington High? Are they checking on Richard and Marty? Did somebody tell them that they saw me at the Purple People Eater with a couple of strangers? And: What do I tell them? Do I act dumb? I can do it.

I've had plenty of practice. Or do I tell them—tell them what? What in the world?

Walking down the corridor to the office, Joe tried to calm himself: there's nothing to fear, nothing to worry about, no need to duck any questions; this is probably about something else, not about the vandalism at all. That's it. It's about something else. His heartbeat settled back into a normal rhythm. His hands quit shaking.

"What's up?" Joe asked the girl.

She shrugged without answering.

The girl paused at the door to Mr. Crain's office and waited for Joe to head in. Then she went on down the corridor, probably to the attendance office or someplace like that.

Joe stepped into Mr. Crain's office. He never had been inside before. He had spent a lot of time in the principal's office at Worthington High, but he never had even looked into the Graham High principal's office until this morning when he and others tried to see the extent of the damage. He barely had spoken to Mr. Crain in his six weeks at Graham High. He had had plenty of interviews with Mr. Benton, principal of Worthington High. But his contact with Mr. Crain had been limited to a few smiling nods and the couple of times Mr. Crain said, "Nice game, Joe," when they passed in the corridor.

The principal was seated at his desk. He was a small, slender man with thinning red hair combed straight back. He looked up but did not stand when Joe entered. The man in the sports jacket and slacks—the one Joe figured to be a detective—was seated in a chair to the left of Mr. Crain's desk. The uniformed policeman was in a chair next to him. The office still showed some signs of the rampage—the broken glass on the conference table, the smashed petty cash box resting on top of a file cabinet, one wavy streak of red paint across a wall. But most of the mess had been cleaned up.

"Joe," Mr. Crain said, "this is Detective Lieutenant Hogan and Patrolman Beasley." He spoke in a friendly, reassuring tone of voice.

But there was nothing friendly and reassuring about the way Detective Lieutenant Hogan and Patrolman Beasley were sizing him up. The detective looked Joe over as if he were a bug that someone might step on for the fun of it, his bland stare telling Joe that he was a nothing and that he'd better be careful or he was headed for deep trouble. Joe had seen the look before. The patrolman glared at Joe out of squinty little eyes, as if Joe were a mass murderer or something. No, the two of them did not appear to be friendly and reassuring at all.

Joe nodded at them in acknowledgment of Mr. Crain's introduction.

They did not return his nod.

"As you probably know," Mr. Crain said to them, still speaking in a friendly way, "Joe is one of the stars

of the football team. Perhaps you've seen him play."
Then he turned to Joe. "Have a seat, have a seat," he
said, indicating a chair to the right, facing the detective and the patrolman.

Joe sat down.

"Yeah," the detective said in response to Mr.
Crain's suggestion that he might have seen Joe on the
football field.

The patrolman nodded without speaking.

Joe felt his heartbeat accelerating again. His hands
felt shaky, and a little sweaty. He locked his hands together in his lap. Then he unlocked them quickly. The
tightly clenched hands looked too much like nervousness. This was no time to appear nervous.

"Joe," Mr. Crain said, apparently noticing Joe's
motion, "let me assure you at the outset that there is
nothing for you to worry about." He paused, then
added, "Just some questions."

Sure, Joe thought. Just a little visit in the principal's
office with a couple of cops after vandals have
wrecked the place. Nothing to worry about at all. Joe
felt himself go on the alert. He had heard the friendly
line before. Please let down your guard for a minute,
will you, so we can zap you. Joe knew the tactic. He
kept his guard up.

Joe said nothing but nodded at Mr. Crain. He
waited.

"You're aware of what happened over the weekend, aren't you?"

Joe nodded again. "Yes," he said. "Everyone . . . "
He closed his mouth.

Mr. Crain smiled slightly. "Yes, I'm sure that everyone knows about it by now, and everyone is talking about it."

"Uh-huh."

"Nobody is accusing you—or anyone else, for that matter—of having anything to do with it, but we are questioning several of the students in hopes that somebody heard something—maybe without even realizing the importance—that may help put us on the trail of the culprits."

Joe frowned and wondered again: Why me? He said only, "All right."

"Good," Mr. Crain said, appearing relieved, although Joe could not imagine what he was feeling relieved about.

Without shifting from the slouched position in the chair, the detective took over.

"Do you have any idea who pulled the break-in?"

"No."

"None at all?"

"No."

"Not even a suspicion? I mean, when something like this happens, a person always thinks—'Ah, that's the kind of thing that so-and-so might have done. I wonder if he did it.' You know what I mean."

"Sure."

"But no suspicions?"

"No, I—"

Mr. Crain turned toward the detective. "Joe is new at Graham High, a transfer student, and probably doesn't know many of the students aside from the football team and some classmates."

"Uh-huh," the detective said. He had a way of making Joe feel guilty. He turned his attention back to Joe. "Have you heard anything—the usual talk among the students—that made you think somebody might know something about the break-in?"

Joe thought of the two boys named at the lunch table in the cafeteria. One of them was Louie Simpson. The other was Henry something-or-other. Joe did not know either of them. He knew only that Paul and Andy—and probably the others, too—thought they were likely suspects. He thought, too, of the nameless boy with the locker next to his.

"No, I haven't heard anything," Joe replied. He spoke without blinking, without changing expression. He did not doubt the honesty of his statement. After all, he did not know either Louie or Henry, and he did not know the name of the boy with the locker next to his. It did not make sense to accuse someone merely because he had heard his name or because of the expression on his face.

Detective Hogan watched him and waited, as if expecting Joe to correct himself. "All right," he said finally, apparently deciding to accept Joe's statement. After that the detective seemed to relax a little.

"Now," he continued, "just as a matter of routine, give us a rundown on your activities and whereabouts Friday night."

The two words at the end—"Friday night"—set off a small alarm signal in Joe's brain. Friday night? How did they know the break-in occurred on Friday night? Why not Saturday night? Or even Sunday night? In his mind he saw again the picture of Richard and Marty with the vodka bottle at the Purple People Eater on Friday night. The detective must know something if he was confining his inquiry to Friday night alone.

"Well," Joe said, "I played in the game against Woodruff."

"I know. I mean, after that."

"I went to get a hamburger."

"With anyone?"

"A couple of friends." He paused before adding, "From out of town. They had come here to see me play."

The detective played the waiting game again, watching Joe. Joe expected him to ask—who, and from where?

But he asked, "Where did you go?"

"The Purple People Eater."

The detective's right eyebrow went up a fraction of an inch. "You hang out there a lot?"

"No. I'd never been there in my life until Friday night."

"How'd you happen to go there?"

"I'd seen it and had heard about it. I didn't know anyplace else to go when we decided to get hamburgers."

"See anybody there you knew?"

"Sure. The inside, and the parking lot, too—the whole place was jammed with kids from school."

"Uh-huh," Hogan said, leaving Joe to wonder what he believed and what he did not believe. "You just had your hamburger and went home?"

"Yes." Joe figured there was no need to mention that he had left his friends in the parking lot and walked home. No need at all.

"You didn't happen to go back to the school?"

"I went past it."

"You did? On your way home?"

"Yes."

"Was that on the way to your house, or did you—"

Joe took a deep breath. Instinctively, he felt a need to be very careful. The route home—and his home address—were easy enough to check. "Not really on the way home," he said.

"Oh?"

"But I knew the way from the Purple People Eater to the school, and the way from school to home, so I took that way."

"Joe's only lived in Graham a few weeks," Mr. Crain said.

"Uh-huh." The detective paused. "What time

was this—when you were going past the school?"

"About ten-thirty or so, I guess."

"Did you see anything—anything at all? Anybody moving around? Or hear anything—noises or shouts?"

"No. Nothing. Nothing at all."

"Ten-thirty, huh?"

"I guess."

To Joe's surprise, the detective suddenly put on a friendly face. He even almost smiled. "Thank you," he said. "That may turn out to be very important. And thank you, too, for answering our questions. Sometimes the smallest details—unimportant to you—can turn out to be very important in the light of other facts we've turned up."

Joe nodded and turned to Mr. Crain.

Mr. Crain said, "That will be all, Joe, and thank you."

Joe got to his feet. He waited a second. Then he turned and opened the door and walked out, closing it behind him.

Alone in the corridor, he took a deep breath and exhaled. No mention of Worthington High. No mention of Richard and Marty. Everything was okay.

But as he walked along the corridor to return to Mrs. Wilde's American History class, the two-word question popped back into his mind and would not leave: Why me?

CHAPTER 15

The question—Why me?—was still lingering in Joe's mind when he entered the locker room to dress for practice after school. He could think of only one answer: His record as a troublemaker at Worthington High had somehow followed him to Graham, and as a result his name had gone on the list of people to be questioned. But Mr. Crain had been so nice and friendly, going out of his way to introduce Joe as a football star, and explaining to Detective Hogan that he was new in town and did not know many people. That was not the way school principals acted when they figured they were dealing with a troublemaker. Joe knew from experience how principals handled troublemakers. And even the detective, though he wasn't friendly at all until the end, never dropped even the slightest hint that Joe's past indicated he was a strong candidate for guilt. So, no, his record from Worthington High wasn't the reason. But if not that, then what? Joe was back at the beginning with the question: Why me?

"Hey, lucky," Andy called out from in front of his locker. "I heard you got called in to give evidence to the cops." Andy was grinning widely as he unbuttoned his shirt and waited for Joe's reaction.

Joe was ten feet away when Andy called out to him. He stopped dead in his tracks. Andy's cheery announcement and broad smile took him aback.

All the players in the aisle between the rows of lockers heard Andy's crack and turned to look at Joe. Some of them were grinning at him. Others were just watching, openly curious about what he was going to say.

Joe had not told anyone, including Andy, about the interview with the detective in Mr. Crain's office. He did not think that anyone knew he had been called in for questioning. The people in Mrs. Wilde's class knew, of course, but they could only guess at the reason. They had no way of knowing that a detective awaited him. Nobody did.

Then it dawned on him. The girl from the office who brought in the note knew, for sure. And she had told everyone that the detective investigating the break-in had interviewed Joe in Mr. Crain's office. The story was too good to keep to herself—Joe Atkins, football star, being questioned about the break-in by a detective. That had to be it. The girl had told everyone.

Joe managed a grin at Andy. "Yeah," he said. "The third degree. But I'm afraid I wasn't much help. It was just—no-sir, no-sir, no-sir, yes-sir, and then back to class."

Joe stepped across a bench to his locker, opened it, and began unbuttoning his shirt.

"Gee," Andy said, "I've never been questioned by a detective."

Joe, who had had plenty of experience being questioned by policemen, gave Andy a sharp look. He wondered what Andy meant by the remark, then decided that he meant nothing. Joe concluded that Andy had really meant it when he called Joe lucky for having been called for an interview with the detective. Yes, for someone who was innocent, and who never had met a detective, the experience might be exciting. "I don't really recommend it," he said.

"What'd he ask?"

"Not much, really. Just whether I knew anything about the break-in, or had heard anything around school today about who might have done it, or whether I suspected anyone."

"Suspected anyone?"

"That's what he said."

The half-dozen players changing clothes around them in the aisle were listening with interest.

With a glint in his eye, Andy glanced at Jason

McNeal beyond Joe and said, "And you told them, sure, you had suspected Jason from the first minute."

"Huh?" Joe said.

Jason looked startled. Then he grinned slightly while everyone else in the aisle roared.

"Or, if you were a real friend, you could have named me," Andy said. "It would have gotten me out of class for a while." His face took on a look of mock seriousness. "If you get the chance, keep in mind that the third period is algebra. That's the one—third period."

"I'll keep that in mind," Joe said, "if the opportunity comes up again."

Everyone laughed again.

Joe watched the smiling faces and listened to the banter and the laughter.

As the noise died down, the question uppermost in Joe's mind came out before he thought.

"I can't figure out why they wanted to talk to me," he said.

Andy shrugged.

With an effort, Joe continued. "I'm not like those guys you mentioned at lunch—Louie and what's-his-name—who are always in trouble, so what do they want from me?" Joe paused. His statement sounded odd to him. If they'd heard it, Richard would have stared in disbelief and Marty would have doubled over with laughter. He paused again, almost expecting someone in the group to correct him. Nobody did.

"And," he went on, "if they just wanted to ask if I'd heard anything, or if I suspected anyone, I'm a pretty poor bet for them. I'm new here. I hardly know anyone, so I'd be the last to hear anything. Why, if I'd actually seen somebody breaking in, I probably couldn't give their name."

"Unless it was Jason," Andy piped up, applying the needle again.

"Aw, c'mon," Jason said. "You've had your joke. This is serious stuff. That kind of talk doesn't do any good."

Andy leered at him.

But Joe knew full well the reason for Jason's concern. First came a few joking remarks, meaning nothing. But the next thing anyone knew, somebody overheard something, misunderstood it, repeated it. Then a teacher picked up on it, and —bang!—there's poor Jason sitting in a chair in the principal's office trying to explain where he was and who was with him. No, Joe understood all right.

"I still don't see why they wanted to talk to me," Joe said.

"They called in a whole bunch of people," Andy said. "They questioned Paul."

"Paul?" Joe was surprised. Why Paul King? He was the straight arrow, the goody-goody who even took it upon himself to tell a stranger he could not smoke a cigarette in the bleachers at the tennis courts. Who could suspect Paul King of anything fishy? Nobody.

So why question him? Then Joe knew the answer. Paul was asked the same questions Joe had faced: Have you heard anything? Do you have any reason to suspect anyone? Joe frowned. The scenario bothered him. Paul may have seen Joe getting into Richard's car. He might have told Detective Hogan, "Well, I saw Joe Atkins, who just moved here from Worthington, with a couple of hoods we saw at the game at Worthington last week—friends of his, I'm sure, and pretty tough characters." And then . . .

Joe involuntarily glanced around, looking for Paul. He did not see him. Paul's locker was in the next aisle, on the other side of the rows of lockers.

"When did they call in Paul?" he asked.

"This afternoon."

"This afternoon," Joe repeated slowly. He silently asked himself a question: Before or after his own summons? If it had been before that might explain why he was called in. If Paul had mentioned seeing strangers with Joe Atkins, the detective might want to question him. But nobody in Mr. Crain's office had mentioned Joe getting into a car with a couple of strangers after the game. The detective had not even asked the identity of the friends Joe had taken to the Purple People Eater. It didn't make sense. But if Paul's interview came after—and not before—Joe's interview, then . . .

As if reading the questions in Joe's mind, Jason said, "The last class, just a little while ago."

"Oh," Joe said, trying to sound casual. But his frown stayed in place. Okay, so it was not Paul's answers that led to Joe being called in for questioning. But what if Paul, going in after Joe, did indeed tell the detective he saw Joe with a couple of tough-looking guys he recognized from the Worthington High game? It would be just like Mr. Goody-Goody to drop that little gem of information on the detective. Hogan just might make a call to Worthington High. He surely would get some interesting answers to such a call. Then he just might want a second interview with Joe Atkins—and summon him anytime, any place.

Joe's mind was swirling.

"Hey, you're really taking this seriously," Andy said.

"What?"

"A guy could trip over your frown."

"Just thinking."

"You've got to watch that—thinking, that is."

Joe got the frown off his face and grinned slightly at Andy. "Just worried about poor ol' Jason, that's all."

Yeah," Andy said. "You ready? Let's go."

On the practice field, Earl Steel hailed the players into a circle around him in front of the goalposts.

"You know who we're playing this week," he said, turning slowly and looking into the faces surrounding him. "The Alexandria Bulldogs are undefeated. Six-oh, same as we are. They won the championship last year, and they want to win it again this year. They beat us 28–7 last year. They know they've got to beat us this year to win the championship again. And we know that we have to beat them to have a chance for the championship. This is going to be a tough game—really tough."

Steel continued to turn slowly as he spoke. The icy blue eyes seemed to drill holes through the players he faced. Joe let the words roll past him. Earl Steel thought every game was tough, and always said so. But Joe kept his eyes on the coach and met his gaze when Steel's slow turning brought them face to face. Joe thought the coach's gaze stayed on him a couple of seconds longer than on the others.

"This is Monday," Steel said. "We've got four days. Just four days. We've got to make every minute count. We've got to work hard—harder than we've worked before any other game. We've got to concentrate—concentrate more than ever before. There's a lot of work to be done. We've got four days—just four days." He paused. "Okay," he said finally. "Let's get to work."

As the players spread out over the field Joe felt the scary question—Why me?—slipping from his mind. He was grateful that the practice session was getting under way. He had to listen to the coaches and understand what they were saying. He had to give his full attention to the plays. He had to run, reach, and catch the ball. There was no time to ask himself again: Why me?

* * *

At the dinner table, Joe's parents asked about the break-in. The news had spread through the town and around the neighborhoods.

"Was there a lot of damage?" his father asked.

"That's what I heard. I didn't see it—just the spray-painting on the walls in the hall."

He chose his next words carefully before he spoke. "They had a detective and a policeman in Mr. Crain's office questioning students."

"Have they got a suspect?"

"I don't know. They were questioning a lot of people." He paused. "I was one of them."

The silence at the dinner table hung in the air and was deafening.

Then Joe's mother said, "You?" Just that, nothing more.

Joe knew the questions forming in their minds. There were too many echoes from Worthington High still bouncing around the Atkins household for a police interview to be taken casually. Beyond that, he had been late arriving home Friday night after the game. He had explained that he stopped for a hamburger with friends. A simple explanation, perfectly acceptable. But . . .

"They were talking to a lot of kids," Joe said. The words came out more easily, more casually, than he had dared hope. "Paul King was called in, too. They were just asking if we knew anything, or had heard anything. That kind of stuff, you know."

"Oh," his mother said.

His father nodded and said, "Uh-huh."

Joe waited. He knew that a year ago this time there would have been a flood of probing questions pouring across the dinner table. Who were you with after the game on Friday night? Where did you go for your hamburger? Where did you go after that? Joe could recite the questions from memory.

But this time his father said, "They'll find out who did it."

And his mother said, "Yes, I'm sure they will."

Then his father asked, "Is Coach Steel cooking up anything special to surprise Alexandria?"

The subject of the school break-in was closed at the Atkins dinner table.

CHAPTER 16

As Tuesday and Wednesday passed, Joe considered calling Richard more than once. The temptation was strong. He wanted to know for sure if Richard and Marty had had a hand in the break-in and the vandalism.

But if Richard admitted it, what then? Was Joe supposed to go to the authorities and turn in his old friends from Worthington High? The idea did not sit well with him. Or should he keep his mouth shut and hope that nobody ever found out that the culprits were friends of his who had come to town to visit him? Holding out on the police or, worse yet, lying to them if questioned again gave Joe an equally uncomfortable feeling. He decided that maybe knowing the truth would be worse than not knowing it.

Besides, what if Richard denied everything? Was

Joe supposed to believe him? True, Richard never had lied to him, at least not as far as he knew. But Richard was not above lying to those in authority—the school principal, a teacher, the police, even his parents. Joe had seen it happen. Richard didn't lie to the pals he ran with, but he did lie to others. And where did Joe fit into Richard's world now? Was he a pal he ran with, or one of the others? Joe knew the answer. After leaving Richard and Marty at the Purple People Eater on Friday night, Joe was no longer one of Richard's friends. No question. So he would not be able to trust Richard's answer now.

So why call him? Whatever Richard's answer, there was no gain for Joe in the call. No, let things rock along. Everything was going okay.

The corridor chatter about the break-in was fading away. It was old news now. The streaks of red paint on the corridor walls were painted over, and the damaged area matched the rest of the corridor. The damage in the administrative offices had been repaired or removed. The students who worked there reported everything back to normal. With the disappearance of the evidence, all reminders were gone. And while everyone knew that surely the investigation was continuing, there weren't any more police interviews with students to feed the grapevine. People were beginning to say that the police never would find the vandals.

Joe, too, was beginning to put the break-in behind him. His mind was increasingly occupied by the same two subjects concerning everyone else at Graham High—the report cards for the first six-week period of the semester, and the impending collision with the Alexandria Bulldogs on the football field.

For the first time in his life, Joe's report card was a happy surprise—three *A*'s, one *B*, one *C*.

He frowned at the *C*—the biology grade. He knew why the grade was a *C* instead of a *B*. He had fallen behind in all of his classes for a few days after being left out of Paul's party. Joe had told himself, "What's it matter?" and left the textbooks unopened. He had been able to make up the lost time in the other courses, but biology was something else again.

Still, the report card was good.

"Richard and Marty would gag at the sight of it," he told himself with a smile. Back at Worthington High, report card day had been different. Joe and his friends always felt themselves lucky to find a single grade as high as *C* on their report cards. They'd boast about how they fooled that teacher, and complained about the others having it in for them and delivering low grades. Joe remembered those sessions, and the ones that always followed with his parents. Now, looking at the card, he decided that this way felt better—a *C* being the lowest, not the highest, grade.

Joe's parents were delighted by the report card.

"You've really got your act together now," his father said. "It's worth the work, huh?"

"Yes," Joe said, and he meant it.

But the praise from his parents brought back the specter of his world crashing down if Richard and Marty were guilty, and if the authorities somehow caught them and linked them to him. What good were the high grades if everyone knew that the vandals had been his friends? What good was the football success if everyone knew what he had been? Paul King, always turning up his nose at Joe, would be proven right. Andy Walker—and Matthew Jefferies and Charlie Janis, too—would vanish from his company. The specter kept returning.

On the practice field, the order of the day was intensity. Joe never had imagined working so hard. Even Andy's ever-present smile was gone, fading away in the face of Earl Steel's constant demands—more, harder, faster, better. Joe gritted his teeth and ran faster, fought harder when a tackler got a hand on him, and reached farther for Paul King's bullet passes. He frowned and nodded when Coach Steel explained the marvels of the linebackers and defensive halfbacks in the Alexandria secondary—a team of powerful speedsters sure to bottle up Joe if he did not work harder, harder, harder.

The buildup to the game, and the grueling preparation, helped Joe to shove Richard and Marty to the back of his mind. On the practice field, there was no time to worry about the streaks of red paint on the corridor walls, or the smashed furniture in the administrative offices. And after practice, in the shower and then walking home in the fading light of the late afternoon, there was too much weariness—and too many bruises—to wonder about who had done the damage and whether their discovery might drag Joe Atkins into the scene.

The upcoming game with Alexandria was becoming the focal point of Joe's world. He even was having trouble concentrating on his homework in the evenings. Visions of linebackers and defensive halfbacks in white and green uniforms kept blurring his vision.

After classes on Wednesday afternoon, Joe was at his locker, stashing the books he did not need to take home, and preparing to head for the locker room to dress for practice.

"Hey, your buddies are okay."

"Huh?" Joe said, turning in the direction of the voice.

The surly looking boy was dumping books in his locker and pulling out a sweater. He straightened up into a slouch and grinned crookedly.

Something in the grin alarmed Joe. Always before, the boy appeared to retreat and almost shrink when he faced Joe Atkins, football star and model student. But now his grin, his whole expression, seemed to convey a feeling of familiarity, almost camaraderie. For the first time the boy was looking at Joe with comfortable ease, as if to say, "I always figured you might be one of us, and it turns out you are. How about that?"

Joe remembered meeting the boy at the Purple People Eater. He remembered the boy's expression. Now he was seeing it again. Joe had been with Richard and Marty, and even though they were strangers in Graham they were easily recognizable in type. They fit in with the crowd at the Purple People Eater. So did this boy. And Joe had been there with them.

"That Marty's a crazy one," the boy said, sounding as if he were delivering the ultimate compliment. "Crazy, really. Richard's okay, too, but Marty's really crazy."

Joe smiled and nodded. It wasn't easy, but he could not think of anything else to do. He wanted to leave. He did not want to talk about Richard and Marty with this boy.

"Where'd you disappear to, anyway?" the boy asked.

"I had to get home."

"Richard kind of had his nose out of joint."

"Oh?" Joe asked blankly. He wanted to run, to get away.

"About you pulling out so early, you know."

"Oh, that. Uh-huh. Well, I had to get home. He knew that."

The boy watched Joe for a moment without speaking. The crooked smile, still there, said more than any words could. Joe Atkins, football star, model student, was, after all, one of them.

"Got to go," Joe said. "Practice, you know."

He turned away from the boy, closed his locker,

twisted the dial on the combination lock, and walked quickly toward the staircase.

All the way to the locker room, and while dressing for practice, the boy's face remained in front of him, the crooked smile seeming to mock.

But once on the practice field, the barking of Earl Steel, the shouting of Steve Howard, the impact of collision, the strain of running—faster, faster, harder, harder—all combined to erase the boy's face and words from Joe's mind.

Walking home after practice, Joe thought again of the boy—but this time without fear or alarm. He thought again of Richard and Marty, of the red paint, of the damage—but this time without fear or alarm.

Finally, everything seemed to be falling into place. Everything was in focus.

And Joe came to a conclusion: If that boy had something to do with the vandalism, it was no business of his. He did not even know the boy's name. If Richard and Marty had something to do with it, it was no business of his. He was not with them. And so what that he had known Richard and Marty at Worthington High?

He was wasting his time worrying. There was no reason to fear getting caught in a snare entrapping the boy or Richard or Marty—if there was, in fact, a snare at all. He was going to wipe the whole matter out of his mind. The important thing for Joe Atkins right now was the Alexandria game. And nothing was going to interfere with it.

CHAPTER 17

"Uh-oh, Louie Simpson," somebody behind Joe said. "Trouble again."

"The break-in, I'll bet," somebody else said.

Joe and the other students milling around in the main lobby before the first class watched the boy, flanked by a man and a woman, turn toward Mr. Crain's office. None of the three looked happy. They did not glance right or left, just straight ahead, as they walked toward the door to the principal's office.

Joe recognized the boy with the locker next to his. "Is that Louie Simpson?" he asked Andy.

"Yep. And his parents. You'll note that they know their way to the principal's office."

"Uh-huh," Joe said.

Once Louie Simpson and his parents were behind

the closed door of Mr. Crain's office, the chatter in the lobby turned to retelling old stories about him. Joe listened with a growing sense of uneasiness. There was the time Louie was caught stealing out of lockers. He had discovered that many students preset their combination locks so that only a half-twirl was needed to open them. Louie went along the rows of lockers making the half-twirl, and a dozen or so of the locks dropped open for him. Three lockers had wallets in them, and he took the money. Then there was the time he was arrested for throwing eggs at a house—Paul King's house, incidentally. And the time he was tossed out of a student dance in the gym because he was drunk. The stories about Louie Simpson seemed endless. And to Joe they had a familiar ring to them—frighteningly familiar.

When Joe came out of his first class and walked down the corridor toward the biology lab, the blue and white police car was parked at the curb in front of the school. Its presence seemed to confirm everyone's suspicion that the topic of conversation in Mr. Crain's office was indeed the break-in. Joe remembered the unsmiling detective in slacks and sports jacket who had questioned him Monday.

By late morning Louie's frequent partner in trouble, Henry Gibson, was supplying details to all who would listen.

"Louie's mother turned him in," Henry said. "His own mother!"

Joe had seen Henry Gibson around school. He was large—not really fat, but big and heavy—with dark skin, dark eyes, and straight black hair. He usually wore the same kind of crooked grin that Louie had, and he had the same sort of shrinking-back mannerism. But now, as the sole source of information about the major topic of the day, he was standing tall, frowning with indignation, and obviously savoring his moment at the center of all attention.

"His mother found a pair of his jeans with streaks of red paint on them," Henry said. "She knew as well as everyone else in town about the red paint sprayed on the walls. So she and his father packed him up with the jeans and brought him to school."

"Were you with him when he did it?" somebody asked.

Henry scowled at the questioner. "Now wait a minute," he protested.

"Just wondering."

I told Mr. Crain and the detective where I was and—"

Joe walked away, heading for his last class before lunch. So, if Henry wasn't with Louie, who was? Surely he didn't do it all alone. There had to be somebody else, too.

The answer began to circulate at noon when Joe, with his lunch tray in his hands, approached a table where a half-dozen football players were sitting.

Paul was talking. "Yes, there were a couple of

others with him, but they're not from Graham," he said. "That's what I heard, anyway."

Joe sat down.

"Where?" Jason asked.

"Where what?"

"Where were they from?"

"I don't know. I just heard that Louie fingered a couple of guys from out of town, and that the police are trying to track them down now."

"Woodruff, maybe. There were some Woodruff people here for the game. And the paint was red . . ."

"Well," said Dave Horton, "you know Louie. He may have just said they were from out of town, and that he doesn't know their names, or something like that. Louie's a slippery one."

"Or he may be telling the truth that he doesn't know their names," Paul said. "You know, he's always hanging around the Purple People Eater, and that place draws all sorts of creeps. You have a few drinks, you know, and everybody is your buddy. He could have picked up with anybody, and it may be the truth that he doesn't know their names."

Joe listened in silence—and with a growing sense of alarm. Louie knew the names Richard and Marty. He had mentioned them to Joe. He also knew they were from Worthington, and that they were old friends of Joe's. So even if he did not know their last names he could say, "Joe Atkins knows them. Go ask him." Would Louie do that? Joe knew the answer before he finished the question. Of course he would. Louie would do anything to reduce the heat, to make things easier for himself. Joe knew the type.

Joe finished his lunch in silence and left the table with a mumbled, "See you later." He deposited his tray on the stack at the door and walked out of the cafeteria.

Heading to class, Joe walked through the lobby. The door to Mr. Crain's office was open. The conference had long since ended. He glanced out the front door of the school. The police car was gone. So, too, presumably was Louie. Joe wondered what they were going to do to Louie. Probation, probably. That seemed the usual thing. But he did not really know. He never got himself into trouble so serious. This was vandalism on a large, and expensive, scale. And there had been thievery. This was serious—really serious—trouble. Serious enough, Joe told himself glumly, for the authorities to go as far as Worthington to catch other guilty parties.

All through Mrs. Wilde's American History class, Joe waited for the door to open. He was sure that the girl who had taken him to Mr. Crain's office and then blabbed to everyone was going to be coming after him. But the door did not open.

By the last period—Miss Churchill's American Literature class—Joe was breathing easier. If Louie had implicated him, he would have been hauled into the principal's office before now. Detective Hogan would have wasted no time calling him in for questioning.

Miss Churchill settled the class down and started a discussion of Cotton Mather's writings of Colonial days.

Joe had the literature anthology open on his desk. Next to it, his notebook was folded back to the page where he had written his homework assignments the night before. He had not enjoyed reading the works of Cotton Mather, but he had done it and was prepared. He found himself actually looking forward to the class. Not only had he done his homework, which made things easier, but this was the last class of the day, and the period of danger was rapidly coming to a close.

Then the door opened and a girl walked in. It was a different girl, but Joe knew the instant he saw her that the mission was the same. Miss Churchill stopped talking. She took the note from the girl, read it, and looked up.

Joe, acting unconsciously, was already getting to his feet.

Surprised, Miss Churchill said, "Yes, Joe, it's for you."

Joe followed the girl out of the classroom and down the corridor. He did not bother to ask her what was up. He knew.

Walking through the lobby toward Mr. Crain's office, he saw the police car parked again in front of the school.

CHAPTER 18

"Why didn't you tell us about your friends from Worthington when we questioned you on Monday?"

Detective Hogan was seated on a straight chair alongside Mr. Crain's desk. He was leaning forward slightly. He had opened the meeting by announcing that Louie Simpson had implicated Richard and Marty, and that they were being questioned at Worthington High at this very moment. And now he wanted an answer from Joe.

Seated in his chair behind his desk, Mr. Crain was leaning back, lightly drumming the arm of the chair with his fingertips. He was watching Joe and appeared uncomfortable.

Joe, erect and tense, was seated in a straight chair in front of the principal's desk. He clenched and un-clenched his hands before answering the detective's question. "I ... I didn't think it mattered. I didn't know ..."

"Didn't know what?"

"I didn't know they were involved. I left them early. I thought they went on back to Worthington."

"You saw them with Louie Simpson."

Joe hesitated. "No," he said finally, "not really."

"No?"

"No. We were at the Purple People Eater, in the parking lot, with a lot of other people. I saw Louie there. But not with Richard and Marty. There were lots of people there." He paused. "I didn't even know Louie's name."

The detective stared at Joe for a full half minute without speaking. Joe returned the gaze.

"Didn't you wonder," Hogan asked, "why we called you in to talk to you on Monday?"

"No, I—" Joe stopped and glanced at Mr. Crain. "I just figured that lots of students were being questioned about whether they had heard anything."

Mr. Crain nodded slightly. "That's partly correct, Joe," he said softly, and then paused. "But your file from Worthington High did indicate there had been some trouble." He paused again and looked even more uncomfortable. "And while you've had no problems here at Graham High, Detective Hogan had thought it might be useful to talk to you."

Joe caught himself glaring at the principal. He tried

to soften his expression. He looked back at the detective.

"You did have a pretty bad record when you lived at Worthington," Detective Hogan said.

Joe nodded but said nothing. He thought he had left the bad record behind, but it was following him.

"Mr. Crain says you seem to have turned over a new leaf since coming to Graham—no trouble, good grades, member of the football team."

Joe did not nod this time. He flushed slightly. So this was what happened when a guy turned over a new leaf. He got himself grilled by a detective about something he had nothing to do with. Was this his reward for sweating at practice, getting bruised in the games, spending his nights at home studying, and staying out of trouble?

Hogan seemed almost to be toying with Joe. Maybe he was trying to make him angry, to trick him into blurting out something that would get him into trouble. Why didn't the detective get to the point? Yes, Joe Atkins knew Richard and Marty. Yes, Joe Atkins was with them last Friday night. But no—no—Joe Atkins did not take part in the break-in at the school. That's it, so long, and goodbye.

"Yes, a new leaf," Joe said finally.

The detective nodded slightly. "Okay," he said, leaning back in the chair. "Joe, I'm going to ask you a few questions, and I want the truth."

"All right."

"Were you with them when they broke into the school?"

Maybe Joe should have seen it coming. Maybe it was a natural, logical—yes, necessary—question. But it stunned him. He felt a wave of panic sweep over him. Was he being accused? Had Richard or Marty or Louie actually put him at the scene? All along, he had been worrying about being linked with them. He had worried about what Earl Steel, Andy, and—yes— even Paul were going to think. But he was so completely innocent of the break-in that the thought of being accused never had occurred to him. The detective and Mr. Crain had seemed to believe he had turned over a new leaf, but now . . .

"Were you?" the detective pressed.

Joe leaned forward. "Did he—did they—say—"

"Just yes or no," Hogan said.

"*No,*" Joe said, a little too loudly.

The detective nodded, keeping his eyes on Joe. Then he asked, "Did you have any reason to believe that your friends and Louie Simpson were planning on any sort of trouble, like vandalism, a break-in— that sort of thing—before you left them?"

"No," Joe replied quickly. The detective did not nod or speak, and seemed to be waiting for something more, so Joe added, "No, not at all."

"Okay," the detective said.

Joe feared one more question: After the break-in had been discovered, did you have any reason to believe that Louie Simpson and your friends might have been responsible? The honest answer had to be yes. But why? Joe had his suspicions, but nothing to base them on but Louie's remark, "Hey, your buddies are okay." But that remark came after Joe had been questioned on Monday. And besides, what was so incriminating about that?

The detective did not ask the question. Instead he repeated, "Okay," and looked at Mr. Crain as if to signal that the interview was at an end.

But the principal clearly had something to say before dismissing Joe. He leaned forward in his chair and picked up a yellow pencil from his desk. Holding it in both hands, he stared down at it for a moment. Then he looked up and said, "Joe, your past high school record raised some warning flags, and that is unfortunate. And your association with the Worthington High boys implicated by Louie Simpson raised more warning flags, and that also is unfortunate. Detective Hogan felt it was his duty to follow up on every lead—that is, look into what's behind every warning flag—and I agreed with him. But let me tell you that nobody here even suspected you of having anything to do with the break-in."

Joe took a deep breath and nodded. But he felt neither relief nor an inclination to believe Mr. Crain. Joe Atkins, with his bad record from Worthington High, was a prime candidate for questions when trouble occurred. It was as simple as that. They had said so themselves, in fact.

"Your record here at Graham High has been a fine one," Mr. Crain continued. "Your record at Worthington High is behind you." He smiled at Joe. "Let's keep it that way, shall we?"

Joe nodded his head and said, "Yes, sir." But other questions were going through his mind. Did Mr. Crain mean that nobody would ever know that he was called into the principal's office again, and why? Did Mr. Crain mean that Earl Steel and Andy and— yes—Paul King would never know? Maybe that was what he was trying to tell him. But Joe knew better. He knew the Graham High grapevine. The word always got out.

Mr. Crain said, "All right, Joe," and Joe got to his feet.

The detective stood, too. Suddenly he was smiling at Joe. "Are we going to beat Alexandria?" he asked.

"What?"

"The Alexandria Bulldogs. Are we going to beat them?"

"Oh," Joe said. He suddenly remembered the football game. "We're going to try," he said.

"Good luck."

"Thanks."

Joe glanced briefly at Mr. Crain, then turned and walked out of the office and returned to class.

Somehow Joe finished the hour of Miss Churchill's American Literature class. He told himself that he should be pleased, relieved, able to relax at last. But he saw only the faces of Marty and Richard and

Louie Simpson, and those of Earl Steel and Andy and Paul—the first three faces representing what he had been, the second three finding out what he had been.

Somehow, after class, he got to the locker room and dressed for practice. He thought that Andy and Jason and some of the others were looking at him in a funny way, like they wanted to ask a question. When they didn't, Joe figured at first that was a bad sign. If everything was open and aboveboard, if nobody felt funny about anything, they would have asked their questions, wouldn't they? Then Joe told himself that his imagination was working overtime.

Somehow he got through the practice session, a light signal drill—the usual routine for Thursday, the day before a game. A couple of times he thought Earl Steel was watching him, really looking him over, in a strange way. He managed to shrug off the thought. Again, probably his imagination. Finally, the practice session ended. He showered, dressed, and left quickly.

At home, his father said, "I heard they arrested a boy for the break-in today."

"Yeah," Joe said.

"Who was it?"

"His name is Louie Simpson."

"Do you know him?"

"I've seen him around."

CHAPTER 19

Word of the Worthington connection in the break-in spread through the corridors of Graham High the next morning. A couple of guys from Worthington High, in Graham on Friday night, had been Louie's partners in the vandalism. Nobody seemed to know where the report came from. And so far, nobody knew the names of the Worthington High boys.

"Do I know them?" Joe asked. "Do I know who?"

"I don't know their names," Andy said. "Just that a couple of guys from Worthington High were with Louie. And, well, you went to Worthington High, so you'd probably know them, wouldn't you?"

Joe shrugged. He was going to play it dumb. He wasn't going to lie, but at the same time he saw no point in revealing that the boys had been friends of his, and in fact were in Graham to see him when they hooked up with Louie Simpson. The whole story was bound to come out one way or another. There was nothing to keep Louie from telling Henry Gibson, and nothing to keep Henry from broadcasting the news up and down the corridors. Or maybe Mr. Crain would tell his wife, who would tell a neighbor, whose son or daughter attended Graham High. Maybe even Detective Hogan—he'd tell a friend, who'd tell a friend, who knew a teacher at Graham High. Joe knew how it went. Everything was bound to find its way into the open. But for now, he was going to play it dumb. And when the word did come out, well, Joe Atkins could be as surprised as everyone else. Why not?

To Joe's relief, Louie was not in school, and available for corridor interviews. As for Henry Gibson, Joe kept walking whenever he encountered him. If any student knew the whole story, it was Henry. And if anyone was likely to blab the news, Henry was the one. Joe did not want to be standing there listening with the others when Henry delivered the news bulletin. So he always kept walking, and he heard nothing.

At lunch, Joe went through the cafeteria line and carried his tray to the table where the football players always sat. As he put down his tray and slid into a chair next to Andy, across from Paul and Jason and a couple of others, the conversation seemed to go quiet. Joe had seen it happen before, plenty of times, back at

Worthington High. The people had been talking about him.

Joe looked around. "What's up?" he asked.

Jason was watching him closely. Their eyes met. Jason was enjoying himself. His lips were curled up in the beginning of a smile—no, not a smile, a sneer. Joe wanted to belt him one in the mouth. He had seen the sneer before.

"What's the matter with you?" Joe asked.

Paul looked up sharply at the threatening tone in his voice.

"Richard Costen and Marty Benton," Jason said, keeping his eyes on Joe. He stated the names matter-of-factly, just letting them hang there in the air.

"What?"

"The guys from Worthington High."

"Oh," Joe said. He felt everyone's eyes on him. He began to eat. Should he volunteer that he knew them? Maybe admit that he knew they were in Graham on Friday night? Even that he had been with them? Then he could express surprise at their involvement in the break-in. Yes, that might defuse things and close the matter for good. But no, better wait and see. He concentrated on his food.

"You know them?" Andy asked.

Joe looked at Andy. The question had a funny sound, like Andy already knew the answer but wanted to hear what Joe had to say.

"Sure," Joe said. "I know them."

Jason was still watching Joe. "Henry Gibson says they're friends of yours," he said.

Again, Joe wanted to knock the sneering grin off Jason's face.

"Yeah, they were, sort of," Joe said. "Back at Worthington last year."

"Are they the guys who were hanging on the fence and hollering at you during the game at Worthington?" Andy asked.

Joe succeeded in grinning at the recollection. "Yeah, that's them," he said. "They're crazy. Always have been. Crazy enough to get in trouble with Louie, too."

That seemed for the moment to knock the inquisitors back on their heels. Jason even looked disappointed at Joe's ready admission.

Then Paul said, "The same guys you got into the car with after the game Friday night?" Paul's expression and tone of voice reminded Joe of the day Paul had leaped out of nowhere and told him, "No smoking on school grounds." Mr. Goody-Goody was scoring again. It might not be Joe's fault that a couple of crazies hung over a fence and shouted at him during the Worthington High game. Or that they came visiting. But Joe had decided to go out with them, and Mr. Goody-Goody obviously disapproved.

Jason's look of disappointment was gone. The glint was back in his eyes.

"Yeah, right," Joe said, and turned back to his

lunch. So Paul had spotted him getting into Richard's car. So what? Let them work for their answers, he decided. Let them have their fun. Who cares? But Joe wondered about Andy. What did he think? The snoots didn't matter. But Andy did.

"And . . . ?" Andy asked.

"And what?"

"Well, what happened?"

"Nothing. I got a hamburger with them and—"

"At the Purple People Eater," Jason interrupted.

Joe glared at him. Jason certainly was feeling pleased with himself. If the snoots already knew it all, why were they asking questions?

Joe swallowed the sharp retort he wanted to deliver and said only, "Yes, at the Purple People Eater, and then I left them and went home. I didn't see them again."

"Lucky you," Jason said in a tone that implied he did not believe him.

Before Joe could say anything, Paul asked, "Was Louie Simpson with you?"

Joe looked around at all the faces turned toward him and felt the anger rising. He clenched his teeth and the jaw muscles tightened. "What is this, a third degree?"

The snap of Joe's words and the fierce glare in his eyes left the table silent a moment.

Then Andy said, "It's just that—"

Paul interrupted him. "What we want to know,

Joe," he said in a low voice, "is whether you're really clear on this thing, or are we going to find out this afternoon that we're playing Alexandria tonight without you."

"You still haven't answered about being with Louie," Jason said.

Paul glared at Jason.

"Cut it out," Andy said. "You're being a jerk."

"I was just wondering," Jason replied.

"Keep your wondering to yourself," Andy snapped.

Joe turned his head to each of the speakers, his teeth still clenched and his eyes squinting in anger. "You—all of you—you think I was with them—a part of it. Well, you can think what you like."

Joe glared at Paul. He was sure he could read Paul's thoughts. Joe Atkins, tough guy, was reverting to form. The boy who broke the rules by smoking on school grounds had fallen back in with his old crowd and had gotten himself back into the old troubles, and he was going to let down the team by getting himself suspended or expelled. It was to be expected.

Joe looked at Andy.

Andy said, "It's just that we're really going to need you out there tonight—to catch those passes and run back the kicks. And ..." He stopped, apparently changing his mind about what he was going to say.

"And you want to know if I've let the team down," Joe finished for him.

Nobody spoke for a moment.

Joe stood and picked up his tray. "See you," he said.

He took the tray to the racks against the wall, dumped his hardly touched food, and unloaded the dirty dishes, stacked the tray, and walked out of the cafeteria.

"Yeah," he said aloud as he walked into the corridor. "The snoots need me—not for their parties, but to catch their passes and run back the kicks for them. They need me so badly they're even nice to me—sometimes."

It was a measure of the Alexandria game's importance that Mr. Crain suspended the entire last class of the day—all fifty minutes of it—for the pep rally instead of the usual last fifteen minutes.

The auditorium was already filling when Joe worked his way through the crowd toward the stage, where the players were gathering to listen to Earl Steel's remarks and the shrieks and cheers from the audience.

"Hey, Joe! Get 'em, Joe!" somebody shouted at him.

Somebody else called out, "Hey, Lightning-foot!"

Joe waved at the sounds of the voices and, unsmiling, climbed the six steps at the side of the stage to join his teammates. At the front of the stage the cheerleaders were jumping around, keeping time to the music blaring up from the orchestra pit. A pep unit from the Graham High band was on hand for the first time.

Joe always felt funny at pep rallies, standing up in front of everyone. It felt good, in a way, when Earl Steel pronounced his name and everyone cheered. But still, he always got a little nervous with everyone watching him.

Joe's first-ever pep rally had been the one before the opening game against Fullerton. Back at Worthington High, he and his old friends had discovered almost immediately that the teachers could not keep track of their students in the auditorium during pep rallies. They did not know who was where or, more importantly, who was there and who was missing. Joe and the others had sneaked out of their first pep rally in the tenth grade, and never bothered to show up at any of them after that. Nobody ever noticed.

Joe looked out over the milling crowd of students and wondered absently if Henry Gibson was among those present or those missing. Missing, probably.

Andy suddenly materialized alongside Joe. "Listen," he said, "about that business—"

"Don't sweat it," Joe snapped.

"It's just that everyone was worried."

"I said, don't sweat it."

Then Paul was with them. "I hope you didn't misunderstand what was said at lunch."

Joe almost smiled. "I don't think I misunderstood."

"We're going to need you out there tonight."

"That's what somebody said."

"And, well, everyone was worried—"

"That's what Andy said."

"Okay?"

"Sure."

Joe looked past Andy and Paul. He saw other players standing in small groups, some of them enjoying the buildup to their moment in the spotlight, others shifting their weight from one foot to the other self-consciously.

Suddenly Joe felt pressed, boxed in by the looming figures of Andy and Paul, speaking so intently with lowered voices. He took a step back from them.

To Joe, Andy and Paul, and Jason and the others, too, all seemed different from himself. He had been mistaken about Andy being a friend. He had been wrong in thinking that Paul was beginning to seem okay. They were all snoots, looking down their noses at him. They needed him because he ran fast and tough, and because he caught passes. But that was all.

Mr. Crain was stepping to the microphone at the front of the stage. Earl Steel was standing behind him, ready to say his words. The cheerleaders were scampering off the stage—half to the left, half to the right. The pep band fell silent. The only sound was the muffled rumble of the conversation in the audience, punctuated by an occasional yelp or cheer.

Paul started to say something, but Joe put up a hand to quiet him. "Don't worry about it," he said, staring into Paul's eyes. He turned away from Paul and Andy and took his place in the row of players.

At the microphone, Mr. Crain leaned forward and said, "Here we are, undefeated, untied, and—"

The rest of his words were drowned out in the roaring cheer that swelled up from the audience and rolled over the stage.

Joe, hands in pockets, stared out at the scene.

CHAPTER 20

Joe ducked out of the pep rally as soon as it ended, skipping down the steps from the stage, cutting back to his right, and leaving the auditorium through a side door. Then, almost running, he went down a corridor to the back of the school and pushed his way through the heavy door. He could pick up his books and jacket from his locker later—or never. Right now he needed to get away. He did not want to see Andy again and listen to more of his bumbling explanations. He did not want to see Paul again and listen to more phony reassurances. He had heard enough from Mr. Goody-Goody. He did not want to see Jason again. At the first twitch of the lip, the first hint of a sneer, he knew he probably would belt him in the mouth, making Jason the victim of what Joe felt about all the snoots, dudes, and heroes he ever had met. Joe turned a corner of the building and walked between the gym and the football field.

The afternoon air was chilly. He wished he had grabbed his jacket out of his locker before going to the pep rally. For a moment he considered returning for it. But he kept going.

He stepped off the school grounds and was turning the corner onto Willard Street by the time the other students started pouring through the doors of the building. He glanced back and then went on.

When he reached his house, he did not go in. He walked past.

It was good to be alone. Alone? He was alone when he was in the locker room with the team, when he was on the practice field with all the others, when he was in the huddle with the offense unit. He was always alone. The other players made sure of it. What he really meant was that it felt good to be by himself.

As he walked, he shrugged his shoulders unconsciously and told himself that they all knew by now—Andy, Paul, Jason, everyone. Probably even Coach Steel. They all knew that Joe's old pals were the kind of guys who went out with Louie Simpson and broke into the school, smashed up furniture, spray-painted the walls, and stole the petty cash. And they knew that Joe was one of them.

They all knew, too, that they had been right when they sized up Joe Atkins at the start. They had been right to stand back from him, leaving him out of everything—the chatter, the jokes, the parties.

Earl Steel had watched Joe in a funny way from the start. Well, Paul King had told him about the cigarette smoking. The coach probably thought that breaking the rules was every bit as bad as Paul King did, so he had wondered about Joe from the start. And now Coach Steel knew he had been right to wonder. Maybe Earl Steel had begun to change his mind about Joe as time passed. Joe had thought so. But now the coach knew his first suspicions had been correct.

Even Andy. Andy always had been friendly. But he was friendly with everyone. And now Andy was sure to be admitting that Paul King and the others had been right all along.

Jason McNeal's face loomed up in Joe's mind. He was wearing a satisfied leer. Jason had been sent to the bench because of Joe Atkins, tough guy. But now that the tough guy's true colors were showing, maybe Jason was going to be in the starting lineup. Joe snorted. He thought again how good it would feel to belt Jason in his smirking mouth. Why not?

Joe heard the words, first from Andy, then from Paul—"We need you." The snoots needed Joe Atkins to win their big game. Well, Joe Atkins did not need the snoots. He never had, and he didn't now. And he didn't need to win the Alexandria game. When had the score of a football game ever mattered to Joe Atkins?

181

When, indeed?

As Joe walked, his thoughts went back one week—to the Woodruff game. Was that only a week ago? With all that had happened, the game seemed a year away. But his first play—the punt return for a touchdown—was clear in his mind. He wanted—yes, *wanted*—to catch the ball, to run, to score. And the week before that, at Worthington, he wanted—yes, *wanted*—to win the game. It was the same in all the other games, too. He *wanted* the Graham Wildcats—his team—to win.

But why? He did not care about the snoots on the team. Joe Atkins *knew* he did not care about the snoots. They did not care about him—except that he could help them—and he did not care about them. Let them play their game against Alexandria.

Joe shrugged. Sure, let the snoots play their game—without him. What did he care? It was that simple. But was it? The pictures kept moving through Joe's mind. He couldn't stop them.

Joe thought of Andy's face when he didn't show up for the game—a frown in place of the grin. He remembered Andy's powerful plunges into the line, always trying for one more yard. He thought of Cramer Springer leveling tacklers in Joe's path on a punt return, and remembered Cramer's friendly greeting the first day of practice. He recalled blowing cigarette smoke in Paul King's face, and then he saw the quarterback scrambling for his life in the backfield, trying to throw a pass to Joe. He heard again the raspy voice of Earl Steel the day of the first full-speed scrimmage: "Young man, I want to see if you're for real."

He thought of his parents. He saw again his father's face at the breakfast table the day Joe's picture appeared in the Graham *Journal*—beaming with pride. He remembered coming home late after the Woodruff game. No questions. No hassle. No frowns. He remembered telling his parents about being questioned by the detective. No hassle. Just some curiosity, then a change of subject. Just smiles and chatter and—well, trust.

Joe stopped in the middle of the quiet residential street. He rubbed his eyes. Everything was so confusing. Then all of the confusing thoughts—the mix of good memories and bad—quit swirling around in his mind. All that remained was one thought, so clear and so right that it surprised Joe. He suddenly saw everything clearly. Life with the snoots, dudes, and heroes was better than it ever had been with Richard and Marty. He liked his new life. He did not want to go back to a life with the likes of Richard and Marty.

Joe looked around. The sun was setting. The hour was late. Too late? He felt a moment of panic. None of the houses around him was familiar. He walked quickly to a corner and stared up at the street signs—Willow and Borden. Willow and Borden? He never had heard of them.

Joe saw a light in a window and walked to the front door of the house and rapped with the brass knocker.

A man opened the door. "Yes?" he said.

Joe felt silly. "I think I'm lost. I was just out walking around, and—"

The man's intent stare stopped him in midsentence. What was wrong?

"Are you Joe Atkins?" the man asked.

"Yes," Joe said, puzzled and feeling a bit troubled by the question. Somehow, admitting that he was Joe Atkins did not seem to be much fun lately. "Why?"

"I've seen you play. I've seen your picture in the paper."

"Oh."

"Where do you live?"

"Six twenty-six Lynden Lane."

"Ooh, you did take a walk, didn't you? That's quite a ways off." He paused. "Wait till I get my jacket and tell my wife, and I'll drive you home. We can't have Joe Atkins getting himself worn out right before the Alexandria game."

"Thanks," Joe said, and the man disappeared into the house for a moment.

In the car the man asked, "Think we'll beat 'em?"

Joe, staring straight ahead through the windshield at the darkening shadows along the street, started to respond with a mumbled, "I don't know," but before he could speak, he heard the same question—"Think we'll beat 'em?"—coming from the detective in Mr. Crain's office. That all seemed years ago, not just one day away. It was the first time a policeman ever asked Joe anything in a friendly manner. He remembered the wild cheers of the crowd for Joe Atkins each Friday night. Nobody ever had cheered Joe before. He remembered the stories in the newspaper—not about a drunk-driving arrest but about victory. He remembered the smiles—instead of frowns—of the teachers.

"What time is it?" he asked.

The man, waiting for an answer to his question about beating Alexandria, was surprised. "Huh?" he asked.

"I think we'll beat 'em," Joe said, catching up.

"It's five forty-five."

"Ugh!" Joe was due in the locker room, stripped of street clothes, dressed in uniform, ready to take the field, at six-thirty—just forty-five minutes away. "It's later than I thought."

"We'll get you there," the man said.

Joe's father let him out of the car at the edge of the school grounds at six-fifteen—late, but not too late. Joe had thanked the man for the ride home, gulped down a sandwich and glass of milk, and hastily grabbed a jacket and accepted his father's offer of a ride, all the while explaining that he had been "just walking and thinking."

"Good luck," his father said as Joe opened the car door to get out.

"Thanks."

"We'll be there for the kickoff."

Joe looked at his father. His face did not look the same as it had looked the night he bailed Joe out of jail in Worthington. "Right," Joe said, and got out of the car, closed the door, and turned toward the school building.

The arc-lights of the stadium were ablaze and the air was full of the brassy noise of the pep band.

Cars already were streaming into the parking lot. People were swarming across the street, headed for the ticket gates. An empty green bus stood parked alongside the school building. The Alexandria Bulldogs had arrived. They were inside, dressing in the visitors' locker room.

Joe trotted across the patch of lawn toward the door leading into the building, weaving through the people milling toward the stadium. He opened the door and stepped inside. The corridor to the locker room was empty. The place was quiet. The silence—the aloneness—gave Joe an eerie sensation. The old feeling of being an outsider among the snoots, dudes, and heroes swept briefly over him, then passed. He walked to the locker room door, pushed it open, and stepped in.

More than thirty faces turned toward him. Most of the players were dressed and the others needed only to tie a shoe or pull on a jersey.

Earl Steel materialized out of nowhere in front of Joe.

"We thought perhaps you might have forgotten," he said.

"I . . . No, I hadn't forgotten."

CHAPTER 21

The other players had left the locker room. They were taking the field for their warmup drills. Joe, hurriedly changing into his uniform to catch up with them, had not watched them go.

"You almost didn't show—right?"

"Huh?" Joe turned in surprise and saw Earl Steel standing behind him. He had assumed that the coach went out with the players.

"I said, you almost didn't show—right?"

"I can explain about being late."

"No need."

"The time just—"

"I said, no need."

Joe stopped with the jersey half pulled down over his shoulder pads. He watched Steel and waited, dreading what the coach was going to say next. Was he going to bench Joe—for being late? For not coming clean about being with Richard and Marty? For something else?

"Sit down," Steel said softly, barely above a whisper.

"But—"

"We've got a minute."

Joe pulled the jersey down over the shoulder pads and his chest. He stepped across the bench and sat down, facing Steel. Steel sat down on a bench opposite him.

For a moment the coach stared at Joe with those cold gray eyes. Joe tried to stare back. He knew now that showing up for the game had been a mistake. He had been right in the first place. He should have left the pep rally and just kept going—going anywhere but here. He should have left the snoots, the dudes, the heroes behind him, to themselves. They never had liked the boy who broke the rules by smoking a cigarette on school grounds, the outsider who beat good ol' chum Jason out of the starting flanker position, the tough runner who knocked the shine off Paul King, the guy with friends who vandalized the school building. The snoots, the dudes, the heroes—they couldn't whip Joe Atkins. So Coach Earl Steel was going to do it for them. Joe clamped his teeth together hard and returned Steel's silent gaze.

"There's only one person on this team who is bothered by your connection with those boys from Worthington, or anything you did when you lived there."

Joe knew he was supposed to ask, "Who?" Then Earl Steel was going to say, "You, Joe Atkins, are the only one bothered by it." But instead Joe said, "What do you or anyone else know about me and Worthington?" He started to add, "What business is it of yours, anyway?" but he didn't. He waited for the coach to admit that Mr. Crain, or Paul King, or someone, had supplied all the tasty details.

If Joe's question caught Earl Steel off guard, he didn't show it. Without blinking, he said, "Oh, I've known all about you and Worthington since the second day of football practice."

Joe opened his mouth and closed it. Then he said, "You have?"

"Certainly," Steel said. He gave Joe a small, almost mechanical smile, and it vanished as quickly as it had appeared. "Didn't it ever occur to you that I might call Coach McCarthy and inquire about the transfer student who seemed to have the strength and the speed to make a football player?"

Joe shook his head dumbly, and his mind flashed back over the early days of practice, trying to find some clue that might have indicated the coach knew all along. He found none.

Steel smiled briefly at Joe again. "I must say that Coach McCarthy gave me an earful—and a bit of a surprise."

"But you never—"

"Never said anything about it," Steel said, finishing Joe's sentence for him. "No, I didn't. Why should I? My interest in you was in your present and your future, not your past."

Joe nodded. He was trying to sort things out in his mind, but the sorting out was not coming easy.

"You don't seem to understand that it is the same with the players, your teammates," Steel said.

Joe had no trouble finding words this time. "They've always looked down on me," he said. Then he instantly regretted the words. Joe Atkins wasn't supposed to admit that anything bothered him.

Steel watched Joe without speaking, and the silence seemed to last forever. Finally, he said, "You've made it pretty rough going for yourself from the start, you know."

Joe remembered the way Paul King had looked at him that first day in the locker room when he recognized him as the boy who had lit a cigarette at the tennis courts. Mr. Goody-Goody wasn't about to like anyone who broke the rules.

"You've thought the players were snubbing you because they had their own friends and you were an outsider."

Joe remembered the early days of practice—all of the players cracking inside jokes that he didn't understand, all of them standing around in groups while he stood alone, all of them looking at him in a funny way and saying things he couldn't hear, all of them worried about good ol' Jason losing out.

"But, to a very great extent, you're the one who kept yourself on the outside. You. It wasn't so much that they were snubbing you as it was that you were snubbing them. You let them know—and no doubt about it—that you didn't care. And tonight you almost proved beyond a doubt that you didn't care about them, or anything."

Sure, Joe remembered fighting back. If somebody cut you cold, you did the only thing you could—you cut them cold first the next time. You beat them to the punch.

"But you're here, and it's good that you are. Now, go out there and play a game of football with your friends, and show them that you *do* care."

Joe swallowed. He wasn't returning Steel's gaze now. He was staring at a spot at the base of a locker beyond him. Steel made everything sound so simple. But things were not that simple. No matter what the coach said, Paul King was a snoot, Jason McNeal was a jerk, even Andy—well, he wondered about Andy and Matthew and the rest of them. Finally, Joe nodded slightly.

Steel stood up. "Okay?" he asked.

Joe stood. "Okay," he said.

Coach Steel put an arm around Joe's shoulder and led him into the corridor and around the basketball court out onto the patch of lawn leading to the field.

Joe jogged away from him and, putting on his helmet as he ran, crossed the lawn to the gate in the chain-link fence at the end of the field. He let himself in and headed toward the rows of players in orange moving through calisthenics.

Maybe Earl Steel was okay. He certainly didn't talk like the teachers at Worthington High who always were lecturing him. Amazing, Joe thought, that Steel had known all along about his troubles at Worthington. Really amazing.

The players were facing Joe as he approached. They all watched him as they bent and straightened. They all knew he had been late arriving at the locker room and that Earl Steel had remained behind to talk to him.

Jason, in the front row, wore an undisguised expression of disappointment. Joe's appearance ended his last hope of seeing most of the action at flanker against the Alexandria Bulldogs. Joe managed a grin at him, just for the fun of it, and Jason scowled back.

"Just one of my friends," Joe said to himself, suddenly aware that there was a lot that Earl Steel did not know.

Andy, in the second row behind and to the left of Jason, watched Joe with a questioning expression. He frowned when Joe grinned at Jason.

"And my best friend is frowning at me," Joe said to himself as he moved into a position at the end of the front and began bending and straightening in the loosening-up exercise.

Paul and Cramer, the Wildcats' captains, were out front leading the calisthenics. It was their turn to watch Joe. Joe gazed back at them with a blank face, revealing nothing.

Earl Steel walked by, heading for the bench. His eyes were straight ahead and looked for all the world like nothing had happened—nothing at all.

Joe kept stooping and straightening, with the roar of the band and the noise of the crowd ringing in his ears.

With the game three minutes old, Joe jogged onto the field to receive an Alexandria punt. The Wildcats, led by Dave Horton at linebacker, had stalled the Bulldogs' first offense thrust.

"Go, Joe! Go, Joe!" somebody shouted from the bleachers, and others took up the chant.

Standing just the other side of the fifty-yard line, Joe wiped his hands on the seat of his pants. Then he clenched and unclenched his fists. He took two steps backward, almost to the forty-five-yard line, and stared straight ahead at the two rows of players on the line of scrimmage awaiting the snap from center.

The kick was high—higher than any punt Joe had seen all season—and deep. He took another step backward, turned his face upward, and watched the ball, a tiny bullet hanging high in the sky.

Finally the ball came down. Joe caught it. He took one step to his right, then another, and two hurtling bodies in white uniforms slammed him to the ground. He had gained five yards on the punt return.

In three downs the Wildcats gained five yards—two on a plunge by Andy, none on a pass to Joe that a defender deflected, and three on an end sweep by Chuck. Ron Sterling came in to punt.

First the Bulldogs and now the Wildcats had learned that there was going to be no easy yardage in this game.

From there to halftime the two teams battled between the thirty-yard lines, neither able to explode for a long gain into the end zone nor to sustain a drive.

The Alexandria Bulldogs had done their homework and weighted their defense against Joe. They knew they had to stop the tough runner with the good hands and the lightning speed if they were going to contain the Graham attack. So they double-teamed him on all pass patterns and blanketed him on running plays. He caught one of the five passes Paul sent his way for a six-yard gain. On the other four passes, there were too many wagging hands around him for the ball to get through. He gained twelve yards rushing on six carries. His longest gain was five yards. He returned four punts, never making more than ten yards.

The other Wildcats fared little better. For Andy, the line seemed an impenetrable wall. His pile-driving plunges netted two, three, once four yards—but never more. Chuck always found a quick linebacker or defensive halfback waiting for him when he set sail around end. His longest gain was six yards. Paul, trying to pass, trying to run, trying to fake, trying to pitch

194

out, was having to operate in the midst of a swarming mass of defenders. There was always a hand on his ankle, an arm on his shoulder, a flashing form in a white uniform blocking his way.

The frustrations of the first half were written on the faces of all the players when they turned and trooped to the locker room for the halftime intermission.

The scoreboard lights read: Wildcats 0, Visitors 0.

Joe passed through the gate in the chain-link fence with the other players, his helmet dangling from his right hand as he walked slowly across the lawn. Andy jogged by without speaking. He had a scratch on his cheek and a small smear of blood beneath it.

Jason came up on the other side. He was not sweaty. His uniform was not dirty. He had been on the field for four plays—the plays after Joe's punt returns—and had carried the ball once for a two-yard loss. His expression when he turned to Joe was almost a sneer. Joe glared back at him, knowing the words forming in Jason's mind: "You're not so hot against a good team, are you, tough guy?" The words were in Joe's mind, and he was sure they were in Jason's mind, too. For a moment he was sure that Jason was going to speak them. But he didn't. He turned away from Joe and jogged ahead of him.

Joe took a deep breath and stared at Jason's departing back. There was an aching in his left hip.

CHAPTER 22

Joe stood between the ten- and the fifteen-yard line, alone.

The second half was about to begin.

Upfield, Joe saw the Bulldogs' kicker placing the ball on the tee for the kickoff. The other Alexandria players were taking up their positions in lines on either side of the kicker, ready to race down the field in pursuit of Joe. Between Joe and the line of white uniforms with green trim were the orange uniforms of the Wildcats, ready to gather at the center of the field to try to burst open a corridor for Joe.

The far goal, beyond the two lines of players, seemed a mile away.

In the bleachers on both sides of the field everyone was standing, silent, awaiting the kickoff.

Joe, clenching and unclenching his fists, watched

his teammates move into position and heard again the words of Earl Steel in the locker room during the intermission.

"We're going to win this game. It's not going to be easy, but we're going to do it. We've got the character to do it. And that's what is going to win this game—character. There will be no mistakes. There will be no letdowns. There will be a lot of determination, a lot of concentration, a lot of extra effort. Those are the things on a football field that add up to character."

The words had surprised Joe and, from the looks on their faces, everyone else, too. Earl Steel never predicted victory. But he was this time. He never delivered those sappy inspirational speeches like the ones in the movie about Knute Rockne that Joe had seen one night on television. But he was trying now to inspire his Wildcats to play the best game of their lives. Frowning as he listened, Joe did not think Coach Steel's words were sappy. He thought Steel was right. The other players were frowning as they listened, too, and some of them nodded slightly in agreement.

Steel's short speech wasn't the only surprise in the locker room. The whole scene had been different. There was no raving and ranting from Steve Howard. There was no cold-eyed criticism from Earl Steel. There were gentle words of encouragement. There were compliments—for Dave Horton for his linebacker play, for Andy for all the punishment he was taking in plunging into the line, for Joe for trying to cope with double-teaming, for Paul for performing under the intense pressure of the hard-charging Alexandria line. And there were the closing remarks by Earl Steel—character, concentration, determination, no letdowns, no mistakes, character. And that was all.

The Alexandria kicker was moving forward. On either side of him and a little behind him, the row of players in white with green trim sprang forward. The line of orange jerseys tensed.

Joe wiped the palms of his hands on his jersey.

The kicker planted his left foot and swung through with his right, sending the ball high and straight, tumbling end over end.

Joe involuntarily took a step forward, his head back, face turned upward, watching the ball. Then he took two steps backward.

The ball was coming down—slowly, so very slowly.

Joe heard the collisions—*whack!*—of blockers and tacklers. He heard pounding feet bearing down on him.

Hands out, he watched the ball. He bent his knees slightly. He was ready, and the ball, finally, was there.

The sound of cleated shoes pounding the ground was louder, closer. Out of the corner of his eye he saw a white uniform approaching. But he had the ball in his hands now and started to tuck it away. The white uniform was coming from his left. Joe wanted to run to his right, away from the white uniform.

But he never took the first step. He never got the

ball tucked away. The hurtling form in the white uniform crashed into him hip high. A pair of arms encircled him. He felt his feet leave the ground for an instant. He felt the ball leave his fingers. He tried to reach for it, but the force of the tackle was driving him the other way, away from the ball. He crashed to the ground. The tackler rolled off him. The ball bounced past, just out of reach. Joe scrambled after it. He pounced. But a blur of white with a streak of green flashed in front of his eyes. The ball disappeared under the blur. Joe landed on the Alexandria player covering the fumble.

Joe got to his feet. The Alexandria player with the ball leaped up and danced around, holding the ball above his head in one hand. A couple of other Alexandria players were dancing around, too. One of them kept pummeling the player with the ball.

Joe was facing the Alexandria sideline. All of the players were jumping and shouting and waving their arms.

Joe saw the referee's signal—Alexandria's ball on the Graham thirteen-yard line.

He turned and began walking toward the Graham bench. He saw the row of somber players standing motionless at the sideline. He saw the defense unit running toward him as they took the field. Somebody patted him on the shoulder and said something as he passed.

Joe walked on toward the bench. He heard the

words, in Earl Steel's raspy, clipped style, over and over again: character . . . no letdowns . . . no mistakes . . . character—*character!*

He felt the tears starting. He was about to cry. Cry? Joe Atkins never cried about anything. But he felt the tears coming. He couldn't stop them.

Ahead of him, the row of Graham High players became faceless, shapeless. Through the tears the arc lights bathing the field seemed brighter than ever. The blur of orange uniforms parted in front of him and Joe, head down, moved through the opening, headed for the bench behind the players. He heard somebody say softly, "He's crying." He wished he could stop the tears. But he couldn't. He finally made it to the bench, sat down, and pulled off his helmet. He dropped the helmet on the ground and buried his face in his hands.

Somebody sat down next to him. "It was my fault," the somebody said.

Joe turned and looked into Cramer Springer's face.

"I had him and he got away from me—the guy who hit you," Cramer said.

Joe shook his head. He wanted to speak but he didn't trust himself to try. Finally he said, "I'm the one who fumbled."

Other players began moving toward them—Paul, Chuck, Andy, Matthew, even Jason, a lot of them—slowly forming into a semicircle in front of Joe and Cramer.

Paul leaned forward. He had a strange expression on his face. For a moment, Joe thought Paul was on the verge of tears, too. Paul leaned his face in close to Joe's and brought down his forearms heavily on Joe's shoulder pads. "It's okay," he said. He pounded Joe twice more on the shoulder pads. "You hear? It's okay. *Okay.* You hear? We'll get 'em."

Joe nodded.

Somebody sat down on the other side of Joe.

Andy leaned in alongside Paul. He reached out with one hand and shook Joe's shoulder pad. "Well," he said, "it proves that you're human."

"What?"

Andy gave a small smile. "I didn't think you ever fumbled. It's nice to know you're just like the rest of us."

"Okay," Joe said.

Nobody said anything else and, in the silence, they heard the silence in the bleachers packed with Graham fans. The silence was bad news. Then they heard a small eruption of a cheer from a corner of the bleachers across the field—the Alexandria fans—and they knew the Bulldogs were punching their way toward the goal.

The players began to drift away from Joe—Cramer, with a slap on the back, and then Andy, Paul, the others—to stand at the sideline and watch the Bulldogs go into the end zone on the third play after the fumble recovery.

Joe picked up his helmet and stood up. He took a deep breath, put on the helmet, and snapped the chinstrap.

On the field, the Alexandria kicker booted the extra point.

Joe looked at the scoreboard: Wildcats 0, Visitors 7.

For the second time in little more than a minute Joe would be receiving a kick and running it back.

Joe started to jog onto the field. Then a scary thought stopped him. He turned and looked for Earl Steel. Maybe the coach wanted Chuck, or even Jason, to receive the next kickoff. Joe flinched when the word went through his mind: character.

Steel materialized in front of him. "What are you waiting for, Atkins?" he snapped.

Joe turned and ran onto the field.

CHAPTER 23

The kick was high and straight, as before.

The ball arrived. Joe heard the fearsome cracking sound of blockers laying low the onrushing tacklers. But he heard no pounding feet this time. He saw no blur of a white uniform out of the corner of his eye. Cramer Springer got his man this time. So did the others. Joe was alone when he caught the ball.

He had it in his hands. He tucked it away and looked upfield. He ran straight ahead, toward the swirling crowd of players at midfield.

He saw a thin opening, a narrow slice of empty space between two orange uniforms. He ran for it. The space widened as he arrived. He ran through.

Something bumped his hip. He kept going. A hand clawed at his right arm, trying to jerk the ball out of his grasp. The hand slid away.

He was at midfield, running in heavy traffic. Suddenly everyone around him was wearing a white uniform with green trim. Then, with a flash of orange, two of the white uniforms fell. Joe ran for the opening.

Skirting the tangle of fallen bodies, he turned on the speed. Clear sailing was just ahead. Then he stopped. Two hands were wrapped around his ankle. The suddenness of the stop almost knocked him off balance. He twisted completely around and jerked his ankle free.

Someone hit him from behind—a jolting blow, high—and he felt hands hanging onto his shoulders. His legs pumping, he dragged the tackler with him.

Then ahead of him—another white uniform.

He could not escape the tackler in front with the load of one hanging on his back. The tackler in front came up carefully and went in low, pinning Joe's legs together. The three of them fell.

Joe jumped to his feet. He looked at the sideline marker to check the point of the ball. Then he turned and looked at the goal, thirty-eight yards away. He never had wanted anything so badly as a touchdown right here and now. But he was thirty-eight yards away.

He turned and started trotting to the sideline. Players were swarming around him. They were slapping him on the shoulder pads. They were cuffing his helmet. They were shouting at him. He heard snatches of words—"beautiful," "great," "fantastic"—above the roar of the cheers rolling down from the bleachers.

The offense unit was coming at him, taking the field.

Paul, in the lead, met Joe's eyes and shot a fist in the air.

Joe, to his own surprise, returned the gesture.

At the sideline, Joe gulped huge breaths of air and watched the play on the field. Paul took the snap, stepped back and handed off to Andy. Andy slammed into the line behind Cramer's solid blocking and, refusing to fall, battled his way eight yards to the thirty-yard line.

Joe trotted back onto the field, replacing Jason. Second down and two yards to go, on the thirty-yard line. This was the closest the Wildcats had come to the Alexandria goal in the entire game. This was the turning point. Joe had seen it in the tenseness of Earl Steel's stance at the sideline. And ahead of him, he saw it in the way the Wildcats gathered for the huddle—briskly, quickly, as if hardly able to wait for the next play. If they were going to beat the Bulldogs, they had to score now. If not, Joe's kickoff return would have been for nothing, Andy's plunge would have been for nothing—and the Wildcats' best would turn out to be too little. Joe no longer felt the weariness. The ache in his hip did not matter.

In the huddle, Paul called the play—Andy plunging straight up the middle. Paul wanted the first down.

Andy got it, fighting his way three yards to the Bulldogs' twenty-seven-yard line.

Then Paul called for a pass to Joe, going deep, slanting across the middle. Double-teamed or not, Joe Atkins was the best weapon in the Wildcats' arsenal. And this was the time to use him. Joe took a deep breath and nodded.

Lining up, Joe stared impassively at the defensive halfback across the line. He felt his heartbeat quicken. He thought of that word again: character. He wished he could trade all of the pass receptions of the first six games for a guarantee of success on this one.

From his left a linebacker shouted something. Joe did not catch the words. The defensive halfback nodded in response without turning his face away from Joe.

With the snap, Joe took four loping strides straight ahead. The defensive halfback waited and watched, and then began backpedaling. Joe lowered his right shoulder to fake a move to the sideline, then cut to his left, turning on the speed as he veered downfield. The halfback almost—but not quite—took the fake. He was with Joe, stride for stride, when Joe went slanting across the field.

So was another white uniform—one of the linebackers.

Joe faked a turn downfield, trying to shake one or

both of the Alexandria defenders, but they stuck with him. Joe shifted into high gear again and looked over his left shoulder, seeking Paul.

The ball was on its way, a rifle shot coming in low. Paul was dancing the nervous little jig that he always did when he tried to thread the needle through a crowd of defenders. Paul became a blur as Joe focused on the spiraling ball.

The ball was there—a perfect pass, waist high.

A hand flashed in front of Joe's face. He blinked. He lost sight of the ball for a split second, but he felt it hit his outstretched hands. He grabbed hard with his fingers. He held on. He tucked the ball away.

The linebacker slammed into Joe's knees. The halfback hit him just below the shoulders. They went down.

Joe got up grinning. He had made the reception. He looked for a yardage marker and found one. He was on the Alexandria twelve-yard line. The play had gained fifteen yards.

A plunge by Andy netted two yards to the ten. Then a pass to Joe cutting across at the goal line failed. The defensive halfback, sticking to Joe like a shadow, batted the ball away.

Facing third down and eight yards to go, Paul called time out and trotted to the sideline. Earl Steel was waiting. Paul, his head down, nodded as Steel spoke. Then he returned to the huddle.

Paul leaned in and called the play—a delayed pass

across the field to Joe running the width of the end zone parallel to the goal line.

With the snap, Joe took off. He ran straight ahead, crossing the goal and going halfway through the end zone. Then he pushed off on his right foot and cut sharply to his left. Turning on the speed, he sprinted the width of the end zone.

White uniforms seemed to be everywhere.

Joe turned. He saw Paul scrambling wildly, trying to elude the charging Alexandria linemen who had broken through the Wildcats' front wall. Paul cocked his arm and fired on the run. The long pass, having to travel three-quarters of the way across the field, seemed to hang in the air forever. Finally the ball arrived. But so did a big hand at the end of a white-jerseyed arm. The hand deflected the ball beyond Joe's reach.

Fourth down—eight yards to go for a first down, ten yards for a touchdown.

Trotting back to the huddle, Joe knew what was coming next.

"Same play," Paul said. He glanced at Andy. "Except—you know."

Andy nodded. "It would have worked last time," he said. "Everybody but the cheerleaders was chasing Joe."

"It'll work this time, too," Paul said.

Joe lined up and, with the snap from center, retraced his steps—a dash straight into the end zone, a pivot to the left, and a full-speed sprint the width of the end zone—this time hoping the defenders would follow, leaving open the spot where he had pivoted.

Making his turn, Joe saw Andy come crashing through the line in a fake plunge. Andy got to his feet and acted like he was looking for someone to block. He drifted to his right, where Joe had come from.

Joe spotted Paul, already having to scramble. Paul was looking at Joe. Then he curled around, eluding a tackler, and lofted a soft pass into the right corner of the end zone.

Joe did not see the end of the play, behind him and across the field. But the roar of the crowd told him that Andy, all alone in the space cleared out by Joe, had caught the pass for a touchdown.

When Joe slowed his run and turned, he saw Andy holding the ball in both hands above his head.

The locker room was a madhouse of shrieks, cheers, whistles and laughter. Even Earl Steel, moving around the room with words of congratulation, had a smile on his face. Everybody was still in uniform and nobody was making the first move toward undressing for the showers.

With Andy's touchdown and Ron's kick for the extra point, the scoreboard lights had shown a tie: Wildcats 7, Visitors 7. But from that moment in the game, the winner had been decided. The Wildcats, cheering each other on, had known it. They walked like winners and they talked like winners. They had whipped the Bulldogs when the turning point came, and they had known they were going to win the game. The Bulldogs knew it, too. They had been whipped at the turning point, and they knew they were going to lose.

In the end, the scoreboard lights showed: Wildcats 21, Visitors 7. Dave Horton had forced an Alexandria fumble and fallen on it in the end zone for one of the touchdowns. Chuck Slater had gotten the other on a twelve-yard run, carrying two tacklers across the goal.

Seated on a bench in the center of the howling crowd of players, Joe looked around and grinned. The victory felt good. His fifteen-yard reception in the first scoring drive had felt good. But what felt best was the look on the faces of his teammates—somehow so different—after that moment on the bench following the fumble.

The snoots, the dudes, the heroes—they were okay.

"Hey!" Joe shouted suddenly. "Where's the party?"

All eyes turned to Jason.

A sheepish Jason McNeal said, "My house."

"Oh, brother!"

Andy, next to Joe, started laughing. Paul King grinned. Even Jason managed a smile. Joe joined in Andy's laughter.

ABOUT THE AUTHOR

Thomas J. Dygard was born in Little Rock, Arkansas, and received a B.A. degree from the University of Arkansas, Fayetteville. He began his career as a sportswriter for the *Arkansas Gazette* in Little Rock and joined the Associated Press in 1954. Since then he has worked in A.P. offices in Little Rock, Detroit, Birmingham, New Orleans, Indianapolis, and Chicago. At present, he is Bureau Chief in Tokyo.

Mr. Dygard is married and has two children.